HER

# Here Comes Ellen

Jean Ure

*Hodder
Children's
Books*

a division of Hodder Headline plc

Copyright © 1999 Jean Ure

First published in Great Britain in 1999
by Hodder Children's Books

The right of Jean Ure to be identified as the Author of
the Work has been asserted by her in accordance with
the Copyright, Designs and Patents Act 1988.

10 9 8 7 6 5 4 3 2

All rights reserved. No part of this publication may be reproduced,
stored in a retrieval system, or transmitted, in any form or by any
means without the prior written permission of the publisher, nor be
otherwise circulated in any form of binding or cover other than that
in which it is published and without a similar condition being
imposed on the subsequent purchaser.

All characters in this publication are fictitious and any resemblance
to real persons, living or dead, is purely coincidental.

A Catalogue record for this book is available
from the British Library

ISBN 0 340 72723 3

Typeset by Avon Dataset Ltd, Bidford-on-Avon, Warks

Printed and bound in Great Britain by
Clays Ltd, St Ives plc

Hodder Children's Books
a division of Hodder Headline plc
338 Euston Road
London NW1 3BH

# 1

Sam and me were upstairs getting ready for bed when the telephone rang.

'Hope it's not Her From Next Door,' said Sam.

We lived in dread of Her From Next Door. Her name was Mrs Pink and she was really crotchety. She was always having a go at Mum about the noise that me and Sam made when we were playing with the dogs, or the noise the dogs made when we put their leads on to take them for walks, or *even* the noise that Felix, our cat, made when he spent a night on the tiles (as Dad calls it).

I squeezed a snake of toothpaste on to my toothbrush.

'Don't see how it can be,' I said. 'We haven't done anything.'

'Don't need to do anything.' Sam

spluttered it through a froth of toothpaste. Gobbets flew about the bathroom. Sam always brushes her teeth very vigorously. She's a very vigorous kind of person. 'Just need to *breathe* and she's on the phone to Mum.'

'I hope it's not Jack and Daisy,' I said. It worried me sometimes, having an old crosspatch of a neighbour that didn't like animals. She didn't like children, either, but that didn't bother me so much. Nobody was going to say that me and Sam would have to be got rid of.

'They only barked just a tiny little bit, when we kicked the ball for them. Like a couple of yips and a hoot.'

It was Jack who had yipped and Daisy who had hooted. Not even Mrs Pink could complain about that. *Could* she?

I heard footsteps up the stairs and my heart sank.

'Mum,' I said, as she came into the

bathroom, 'if that was Mrs Pink—'

But it wasn't Mrs Pink.

'It was someone from Social Services,' said Mum. 'They want to know if we can take in a short-term foster as an emergency.'

'What, now?' I said.

'Yes. Right away. I said we could.' Mum hesitated. 'I hope that's all right with you two?'

Wow! She was actually consulting me and Sam!

'If it isn't, we'll just take her for tonight and they'll have to find somewhere else for her tomorrow. What do you think?'

'Sounds all right to me,' said Sam.

'Abi? How about you?'

'Mmm.' I nodded. I had my mouth full of toothbrush.

'Are you sure?' Mum looked at me, doubtfully. 'It would mean you and Sam sharing a room for a few weeks. How would you feel about that?'

I frowned, as I rinsed my toothbrush under the tap. Right back at the beginning, when Mum and Dad had first decided to foster, they'd promised me the one thing I would never have to do would be to share my bedroom. I wouldn't normally have had to, only my nan was staying with us in the room we kept for spare.

'Say if you'd rather not,' said Mum. 'They can always find her somewhere else.'

I wrestled with my conscience. Was it so much to ask? Just sharing my room for a few weeks?

'No. It's all right.' I shook my toothbrush dry and put it back in its holder. 'I don't mind if Sam doesn't.'

'Sam?'

Sam humped a shoulder. 'All the same to me.'

'So I'll tell them she can stay for the full three weeks? Whatever it is. You're quite sure about it?'

'Yeah! It'll be fun,' said Sam.

I wasn't quite sure that I thought it would be *fun*. I suppose I have been a bit spoiled, being an only child for the first ten years of my life and never knowing what it's like to share. I really enjoy having my bedroom to myself! I like being in my own space, with my things all ranged around me. On the other hand, Sam and me are really close; we're the superglue kids, we do everything together. Have no secrets, tell no lies. We are like real sisters! Better than real sisters. Real sisters quarrel, but me and Sam never do. Well, almost never.

If I had to share my room with someone, I'd sooner it was Sam than anyone else.

'Come on, then!' said Mum. 'We'd better get moving. They'll be here any minute.'

We didn't have a spare bed (apart from the one that Nan was sleeping on) so Mum said we'd make one out of mine by using the mattress.

'One of you can be on the top half, one on the bottom.'

'I'll have the bottom bit,' said Sam, generously. The bottom bit was the hard bit.

'We ought to take it in turns,' I said. But Sam insisted. She said that she was bigger than me and wouldn't feel it so much.

The Radish came stumbling out of his room while we were making up the beds. (We call him the Radish because of his surname being Radice, pronounced Rad-ee-chay. His real name is Gus. We were hoping that one day we would be able to adopt him and then he would be called Foster like me and Mum and Dad. Sam can't be adopted but she is with us long-term so it is almost the same.)

'Wot'th happ'ning?' said the Radish. He'd lost some of his front teeth and it made him lisp. He was only seven.

'Me and Sam are going to share my

bedroom 'cos we've got a new foster coming,' I said.

The Radish stuck his thumb in his mouth and his eyes went all big and owly.

'Coming now?'

'Yes! Immediately.' It suddenly struck me. 'Why does she have to come in the middle of the night?'

'Because her mum's just been rushed into hospital and there's no one to look after her.'

'How old is she?'

'What's her name?'

'Where's she live?'

'Where's she go to school?'

Me and Sam bombarded Mum with questions.

'She's fourteen,' said Mum. 'Her name's Ellen. Ellen Dredge. She—'

'Ellen *Dredge*?'

We chorused it together. Mum looked at us, sharply.

'All right! We don't need any smart remarks. She didn't choose her name.'

I pulled a face. 'Where does she go to school?'

'She goes to your school, as a matter of fact. That's one of the reasons they asked if we could take her.'

I hadn't ever heard of anyone called Ellen Dredge at our school but of course she would be in the Seniors. Sam and me were top Juniors. We're on the same site, but different buildings.

'She's Special Needs, by the way. So you'll have to be prepared to make allowances.'

'Just hope she likes dogs,' said Sam.

The Radish had been terrified of them, just at first. They'd had to be shut away. And they're only little! I didn't want to go through that again. Jack *hates* being shut away. (Jack is my dog. Daisy is Sam's.)

'Mum,' I said, anxiously, 'did you check? You said in future you'd check!'

'Abi, I'm sorry, I didn't have time,'

said Mum. 'It all happened so quickly. But I'm sure she'll be fine.'

Dad and Nan had come upstairs to see how we were getting on.

'Anything I can do?' said Dad.

When Mum said no, he gave a big sigh of relief and went back downstairs again to the telly.

Nan said, 'Reen, are you sure this is sensible?' Reen is my mum's name. Short for Doreen.

'Probably not.' Mum said it cheerfully. 'But what could I do? The poor child's just seen her mother taken away in an ambulance. She needs somewhere!'

'I'd have thought two were enough,' said Nan.

She meant Sam and the Radish. But we don't look on Sam and the Radish as fosters! They are family.

'Not to mention' – Nan muttered it darkly – 'all those animals.'

All those animals? We've only got three!

'Oh, it'll be all right.' Mum cast a quick glance round Sam's bedroom. It looked rather bare with most of Sam's stuff taken out. 'We all muck in. Gus, back you go to bed! And you two girls.'

'Can't we stay up and see her?' begged Sam.

'I think it would be better if you waited till morning. She's bound to be a bit confused and upset. You can meet her at breakfast. Go on, now! Off you go. And no peeking through the banisters!'

Sam and me pulled faces but obediently trundled off. Jack and Daisy came with us. They got really excited when they found my bed split into two with the mattress on the floor! Daisy immediately flung herself on to her back and Jack started trying to burrow his way underneath it. Sam and me left the light on and sat up to talk. We had absolutely *no* intention of going to sleep and missing out on the excitement!

'Fourteen,' said Sam. 'That'll be Year 9.'

We didn't have anything to do with Year 9s. Well, they didn't have anything to do with us. To them I daresay we were just babies. Silly little tiddlers, not worth bothering with.

'I don't expect we'll see much of her,' I said.

'Wonder what's wrong with her mum?'

'Dunno. Burst appendix, maybe.'

It was the only thing I could think of that would make a person have to be suddenly rushed into hospital. Well, that or a heart attack, but I didn't think Ellen's mother could be old enough for heart attacks.

I giggled. 'Ellen Dredge! What a name!'

'Better not let Mum catch you saying that. Remember how mad she used to get about the Radish?'

Mum had been furious with me and Sam when we'd started calling Gus the Radish. She'd thought we were making fun of him, but we weren't. It wouldn't have been fair to make fun of anyone as weedy and scaredy as the Radish had been when he first came to us. He's still pretty weedy but at least he's not so scared any more. Just a bit nervous on account of all the bad things that have happened to him in his life. And he's quite proud of his nickname! Sometimes he even refers to himself as 'Waddish'.

I sat on my pillow with my legs crossed, wondering what Ellen Dredge would be like. I hoped she wouldn't give herself airs and graces, being a Year 9. Year 9s can be really snooty. And some of them can be a bit frightening. Some of the bigger, tougher ones. Not just the boys; girls, as well. They fight and swear and do drugs. I've seen them.

I suddenly started to worry in case the Ellen Dredge person would turn out to be like that. She might be unkind to the animals!

I think I must have looked worried or been

munching my lip or something 'cos Sam suddenly said, 'Abi, I won't mess your things up. Honest!'

I slewed my head round to look at her. What things? What was she talking about?

'Your *things*,' said Sam. She waved a hand about the room.

'Oh! My things. That's all right,' I said.

All my clothes had had to be squashed up in one half of the wardrobe to make room for Sam's, but that didn't bother me. I am not terribly into clothes, to tell you the truth. I mean, I like to look nice but I am not always nagging at Mum to buy me the latest gear. I am usually covered all over in dog hairs, anyway! Some people go 'Ugh' and 'Yuck' and 'Horrible!' but I just say, 'So what?'. They brush off.

Most of them. Sometimes.

Well, anyway, I don't care! I'd rather have Jack and be covered in dog hairs than not have him and look like a doll, like a girl in our class called Mary-Jo Mitchell, who is one of the worst ones for going 'Ugh' and 'Yuck'.

'Sorry about your ornaments,' said Sam.

I have lots of little china and glass figures which had had to be crammed on to one shelf so that Sam could have the other one, and my dolls' house had had to be shoved into a corner, which I didn't like very much as it meant I couldn't get at it, but I reminded myself that it was only for a few weeks and that Ellen Dredge's mother had been taken to hospital in an ambulance and we had to feel sorry for her.

(I don't actually *play* with the dolls' house, by the way. What I like to do is decorate it and make things for it. That is quite different from playing with it.)

I spoke my thoughts out loud and said, 'After all, it's only for a few weeks.'

'Yes, but I know you like things tidy,' said Sam.

'Well, I do,' I agreed.

'And Mum is always saying how my room looks like a bomb's hit it.'

'Yes.' I sighed. I really hated not being able to get to my dolls' house. I like to leave the front open so's I can gloat over all the little bits of furniture I've made and the different patterned papers I've put on the walls. I like to dream up new colour schemes and think of new ways of arranging the rooms. I am seriously into this sort of thing. It is what I am going to do when I grow up.

But it was only for a few weeks! Surely I could put up with Sam and her untidiness just for a few weeks?

'It's a pity it had to happen when Nan was here,' I said. My nan lives way up north so when she comes to visit she always stays at least a month. And this was only her second day! 'If it had been any other time, we'd have had room.'

'Yeah.' Sam wiggled her toes, then

screeched as Daisy pounced on them. 'Pity she can't sleep in the attic.'

'Who, Nan?' I was startled. Nan was old! She'd never get up the attic stairs.

'No! This Ellen person.'

'Dad was going to turn the attic into a proper bedroom, once, but then he reckoned we'd got enough without it.'

'Got more'n most people,' agreed Sam.

We have. We have *five*! Five bedrooms. Can you imagine? But in case anyone is thinking to themselves that we must be immensely rich and wondering if maybe we have won the lottery, I will just say that we are not in the least bit rich and nor have we won the lottery, alas! The house was left to Mum by her Auntie Marge. Before then there was just me, and Mum and Dad, and of course Jack and Felix, living cheek by jowl (as the saying goes, though I'm not quite sure what it means) in a teeny weeny little flat. Sometimes even now, when I go chasing up the stairs and along the passage with Jack, I can't quite believe that we have so much space! Even with the addition of Sam and Daisy and the Radish, we can move around without bumping into one another. And it is all thanks to Auntie Marge!

'Did Mum say where this Ellen person lives?' I said. 'Did she—'

'Shh!' Sam put a finger to her lips. 'I can hear something!'

We sat there, listening. The dogs listened, too. Then Jack barked – just once, very loud and shrill. A car had pulled up outside. (He thinks he owns the street, does Jack! He always barks at cars.)

'It's her!' Sam scrambled off the bed. 'Let's go and see what she looks like!'

Mum had told us we weren't to peek through the banisters, but she hadn't said not to look out of the window. We rushed across the landing into Mum and Dad's room, which is at the front of the house. We saw a woman coming up the path, followed by a large, lumpish-looking girl wearing a quilted anorak ('Yuck!' said Sam) and saggy blue jeans all bagged and shapeless.

'Snazzy dresser,' whispered Sam.

I jabbed her in the ribs.

'Quiet! She'll hear you.'

Mum and Dad always keep their bedroom window open, even in winter. We were in March, now, and it was quite warm.

We watched the girl as she shambled up the path. She had this big moon face, very puffy and pale. I thought that probably the reason it was puffy was that she'd been crying. I know I'd cry if my mum was taken off to hospital. I'd weep buckets. And anyone would look pale in the gloomy orange glow of the street lamps. It wasn't fair to judge her by one quick glimpse as she came up the path.

Sam and me crept back along the passage. We heard Mum say, 'Ellen? Is this Ellen? Come on in, luvvy! Come and have some hot chocolate. We'll soon get you comfortable.'

It was a temptation to take a quick peek through the banisters, but we were scared that Mum might catch sight of us so we scuttled sideways like crabs into the safety of our room.

'Well!' Sam thumped herself down on to her hard bit of bed. 'What d'you reckon?'

'She did look a bit odd,' I said. 'But I expect she'll look better in the morning.'

# 2

Me and Sam were out of bed next morning before my alarm clock had even stopped ringing.

This is almost unheard of! What usually happens, the alarm rings and I turn it off then I snuggle down again underneath the duvet and go back to sleep and wait for Mum to call me. Sometimes she has to call me three or four times before I manage to un-gum my eyes and wake up. She can get really ratty about it.

'Abi!' she yells. 'Sam!' ('Cos Sam is just as bad.) 'I am not calling you again!'

Today she didn't even have to call us once. We rushed into the bathroom, splashed some water over our faces, rushed back to the bedroom, tore into our clothes and catapulted down the stairs, almost falling over the dogs on our way. They weren't used to such hectic activity so early in the morning!

Mum was quite surprised when we came bundling into the kitchen.

'Well, look who it isn't!' she said.

This is a strange expression that she uses. I have *never* understood it.

'You've just missed your dad. He had an early call.'

Dad's a plumber. People call him out at the oddest times. And for the oddest things! Once an old lady rang him in the middle of the night 'cos she said her central heating was making gurgly noises and she couldn't get to sleep. Dad told her to put some cotton wool in her ears and he'd be round in the morning. But he did it quite politely, 'cos he's like that, my dad.

'What's got you two up so bright and early?' said Mum.

'Just felt like it,' said Sam. Her eyes flickered about the kitchen, checking all the possible hiding places. Under the sink . . . in the cupboards. 'Where is she?' she hissed.

'Where is who?' said Mum.

'*Her.*' Sam mouthed it, not quite saying it out loud. I nearly giggled. She couldn't really think Ellen was hiding from us in a cupboard?

'If you mean our new guest,' said Mum, 'she does have a name. I believe I told you what it was.'

'Ellen,' I said.

Ellen Dredge. But it wasn't her fault. She couldn't help it.

'Is she still in bed? Shall we go and get her up? We wouldn't want her to be late for school,' I said, virtuously.

'I'll give her a call in a minute,' said Mum. 'Who's this?'

The door had opened, just a crack, and the Radish came sidling through.

'Another early bird,' said Mum. 'How amazing!'

'Ith thee here?' whispered the Radish.

'Her name's Ellen,' I said. 'She's not up yet.'

'Thall I go an' get her?' offered the Radish.

He was halfway out of the door before Mum dragged him back.

'Just leave her. She had a lot of upset last night.'

'But, Mum,' I wailed, 'she'll be late for school!'

'You'd probably be late for school if I'd been carted off to hospital,' said Mum. 'We'll let her w—'

Mum broke off. Heavy footsteps were clumping down the stairs. THUD. Bang. Crash! *Wallop*. I saw Mum wince slightly. Me and Sam exchanged glances. Was this girl wearing hobnailed boots?

The door crashed open and Ellen came in. She was dressed in school uniform; grey skirt and jumper, same as me and Sam. Her face was very big and round but it didn't look puffy any more, so maybe she'd stopped crying, or maybe it had just been the street lights.

'Ellen!' said Mum. 'Did you have a good night? Did you get any sleep?'

'I slept *orrrrrrrrrrrrrrlll* night,' said Ellen.

She really did say *orrrrrrrrrrrrrrrlll* night. It went on for ever. We just kind of stood there, frozen, waiting for her to finish.

She wasn't very pretty. Her face was too big and her eyes were too small and her hair was all messy. But she had lovely pink cheeks that I really envied, 'cos mine are the colour of pastry. And when she finally stopped saying *orrrrrrrrrrrrrlll* and broke into this big smile, you had to smile back 'cos she looked dead impish!

Mum said, 'Ellen, let me introduce you. This is Abi . . . this is Sam . . . and this is Gus.'

Ellen said, 'Hello, Abi! Hello, Sam! Hello, Gus!' Each time she said hello, she held out her hand. I thought it would be all cold and fishy but in fact it was quite nice and warm and soft. I was surprised about that.

'And this is Jack,' said Mum. 'And this is Daisy.'

Ellen said, 'Hello, Jack! Hello, Daisy!' And she picked up their paws and solemnly shook them, just as if they were people. So then I felt bad about thinking she might feel fishy. Anyone who gets on with animals is OK with me!

'You met Felix last night,' said Mum.

Felix was crouched in his favourite spot, on top of the fridge, silently watching us.

'Hello, Felix!' said Ellen. And guess what? She goes and takes one of Felix's paws! If there's anything Felix hates more than anything else, it's having his paws touched. I expected him to yank it crossly away, but to my surprise he patiently waited until she let go, then frantically began licking at it. Truly amazing! He was obviously in a good mood.

'And this is Nan,' I said, as the door opened.

Ellen immediately said, 'Hello, Nan!' and held out her hand. It was like she was programmed or something.

Nan blinked and said, 'Hello, my dear! How are you this morning?'

Ellen flung out her arms. 'I am *orrrrrrrrrrrrrrrrlll* right, thank you!'

'Well, that's good,' said Nan.

We sat down to breakfast.

'Ellen, I'm doing you a boiled egg,' said Mum. 'Do you like boiled eggs?'

'I *adore* boiled eggs,' said Ellen. And she flung out her arms again and sent the milk jug crashing to the floor.

'Don't worry, don't worry,' said Mum. 'Sam? Abi? Can you mop that up for me?'

Down on our knees on the kitchen floor, me and Sam looked at each other. If that had been one of us had sent the milk jug flying, we wouldn't have got away so lightly! It would have been, 'Now look what you've done' or 'For goodness' sake, you two! Stop messing about'. But Ellen was a guest. Guests were treated differently. Sam had been a guest, once; so had the Radish. Now they were members of the family and got bawled out, same as me. Not that Mum bawls a *lot*. Just now and again when we do something extra-specially annoying and really 'get on her wick' (another of the curious expressions she uses).

We all sat round the kitchen table, me and Sam, Ellen and the Radish, with Nan at one end and Mum at the other. Mum put the boiled eggs out. Me and Sam and the Radish all have our own ways of eating eggs. Sam likes to bash hers with a spoon and take the top off. I like to crack mine, but quite gently, and then pick at it. The Radish likes to make a tiny little hole and dip, with toast fingers. Ellen – well! She didn't seem to have any idea. First she gets her spoon and starts whacking. She whacks so hard she shatters the thing and the whole top caves in. Egg yolk goes splattering everywhere, all over her plate, all over the table, all over her school tie.

Next she wants to dip toast fingers, like the Radish, only she hacks her toast into little pieces so that she can't dip them in the yolk without dipping her fingers as well. She's a really messy eater! She ends up with yolk round her mouth, yolk on her tie, yolk on her sweater. Little drippy blobs of it, all down the front.

It's the Radish that draws attention to it.

'Ellen'th thpilt egg on herthelf!'

Ellen looks down at her sweater and goes 'Oops!' and giggles. Next thing we know, she's stuffing it into her mouth, trying to suck it clean. Yeeurgh! I try not to look. It makes me feel sick. Sucking her *sweater*.

Mum says, 'Ellen . . .' but Ellen's slurping at her tie now, and Mum's voice fades away into helplessness. Nan takes charge of the situation. She goes over to the sink, squeezes out a cloth, and says very firmly to Ellen, 'Let's sponge that off, dear, shall we? Else it'll mark.'

Sam catches my eye and pulls a face. I know what she's thinking. This girl is *fourteen*. She's a Year 9. What is the matter with her?

Me and Sam were quite used to taking the Radish into school. The Infants was in the same road as the Juniors, so we always left him at the gates and collected him again on the way home. We hadn't expected that we would have Ellen lumping along with us!

'Can't she go by herself?' Sam hissed.

'Not on her first day,' Mum said. 'She might get lost.'

It turned out that Ellen lived on the other side of town. Only ten minutes away from school, but in quite the opposite direction. So there we were, stuck with her. I didn't know what to talk to her about! I mean, she was loads older than we were, but she seemed so . . . *childish*. It was because of being Special Needs; I knew that. But I still couldn't think what to talk about!

It was Sam, as usual, who found something to say. Sam is almost never at a loss.

'What year are you in?' she said.

'Year 9, Year 9, I'm in Year 9!' Ellen began jumping on and off the kerb. 'Year 9, Year 9, I'm in Year 9! Year 9, Year 9—'

'Who's your class teacher?' said Sam, hurriedly.

'Mr *Steeeeeeeeevenson!* Mr *Steeeeeeeee-venson!* Mr *St—*'

'Is he nice?' I said. This was awful! People were looking at us.

'He's very nice, he's very nice, he's very very very—'

'You'd better stop that,' said Sam, 'or you'll get run over.'

'*Radish!*' I grabbed him just in time. 'Don't you start!'

All the way to school Ellen was hopping

and chanting. I know it wasn't doing any harm. And she was happy! But it was dead embarrassing. I couldn't help feeling relieved when we finally arrived at school and could part company. We gave Ellen a little push in the direction of the Seniors and scurried thankfully off through our own entrance.

'See you later!' I called.

'See you later, alligator!' Ellen stood there, flapping her hand. She was still flapping it when I looked back, a few seconds later.

'She's a bit of a pain, isn't she?' said Sam.

I swallowed. 'I s'pose she's just a bit . . . young for her age.'

Mary-Jo Mitchell and her best friend Lissie Thomas were lying in wait for us.

'Who was that?' said Lissie.

They must have seen Ellen, skippity-hopping on and off the kerb.

'Oh! Just someone,' I said. 'She's staying with us,' I added.

They were bound to find out. They always

found out everything, those two.

'Looks a bit loopy to me,' said Mary-Jo.

Sam thrust out her chin, pugnaciously. 'What do you know about it?'

'She was dancing,' I said.

'That's right,' said Sam. 'She was dancing.'

We linked arms and went marching off along the corridor.

'Funny sort of dancing!' yelled Mary-Jo.

We didn't expect to see Ellen again until after school. Hopefully not until we got home at four o'clock . . .

During dinner break we were in the playground, throwing a ball around with Mary-Jo and Lissie Thomas and one or two others. Sam is in the Under-11 netball team and so are Lissie and Mary-Jo. They are really keen. I am not, terribly; in fact I am absolutely useless at games. But Sam and me always do things together, so if she wanted to practise netball I had to go along with it.

'Pass! Pass!' cried Sam.

I quickly threw the ball at her. (I always like to get rid of it as soon as possible.) Sam threw it to Lissie, who threw it to Mary-Jo. And then, right slap into the middle of us came this large lolloping figure . . . Ellen! What was she doing here? This was the Junior playground! Seniors never came into it.

'What do you want?' said Sam.

Ellen beamed. 'I came to find you.'

'But this isn't your playground!'

'No,' said Ellen. She gave a little giggle. 'I know!'

'So don't you think you ought to go back to your one?'

Ellen shook her head. She didn't want to go back to her one! She wanted to stay and play netball with us.

She made the most terrible nuisance of herself. She kept jumping up and pushing at the ball. She bashed into people. She lumbered in front of them so they couldn't run properly. Everyone kept shrieking at her to 'Get out the way!' but it was like she didn't even hear them. She just went on grinning and lolloping, until in the end Mary-Jo screamed, 'Look, if you want it, have it!' and she slammed the ball straight at her, quite hard.

Ellen thought that was really funny. Or maybe she thought it was all part of the game. She caught the ball and went loping off round the playground, hugging it to herself and chanting as she went: 'Ball snatcher, ball snatcher, here comes the ball snatcher!'

'She is *totally* loopy,' said Mary-Jo.

'She's not loopy,' snarled Sam. And then under her breath she muttered, 'Just a pain.'

I looked at Mary-Jo, reproachfully. 'She's Special Needs,' I said.

'So? I don't see why we should have to put up with her!'

Making like it was *our* fault.

At the end of school we went to fetch the Radish, same as usual.

'Where'th Ellen?' he said.

'Don't know and don't care!' snapped Sam.

When we got home Mum said, 'You didn't wait for her?'

I crinkled my forehead, resentfully. 'Were we meant to?'

'Well, it would have been nice. All things considered.'

'You should have *said*. If you'd *said*, we'd have *done* it.'

'I was rather hoping I wouldn't have to. After all, it is her first day.'

I heaved a sigh.

'I did tell you,' said Mum. 'You have to be prepared to make allowances.'

I know it was uncharitable, but I didn't feel like making allowances. She was such an embarrassment!

'Does it give you any problems?' said Mum.

Glumly, I shook my head.

'Sam, how about you? Does it give you any problems?'

'Me?' Sam started, guiltily. 'No!'

'You're sure?'

'Yeah! I mean – yeah. Way to go!' said Sam.

She comes out with the weirdest expressions. I asked her later what it meant, and she said she didn't know! It was just something she'd heard on the telly. But anyway, as I reminded her, it was *only for a few weeks*.

'Not like it's a lifetime's sentence.'

Sam just rolled her eyes.

By five o'clock Ellen still wasn't home and Mum was beginning to get worried. Well, I suppose we all were. I suppose Sam and me felt a tiny bit guilty. Not because we hadn't waited for her – I mean, we *would* have done if Mum had *said* – but 'cos of getting mad at her. She couldn't help being young for her age and an embarrassing nuisance. We certainly wouldn't want anything bad to have happened to her.

And then, just as Mum was getting really fussed and wondering whether she ought to ring the police, there was a knock at the door and there was this woman with Ellen. She had found her wandering in Hop Hill Road! Hop Hill Road is miles away.

Ellen came bounding through the door. She didn't seem any the worse for her experience.

'Abi!' she cried. 'Sam!' And she galumphed across the room and flung her arms round us. *Dead* embarrassing.

'What happened to you?' I said.

'I got lost!' Ellen did a little twirl and knocked over a chair. She was really clumsy. Worse even than me. 'This lady brought me home in her car. She was s-o-o-o nice!'

'But even the Radish couldn't get lost just walking home from school,' I said. 'All you have to do is just go down Valley Road, cross over at the bottom, turn right, walk along the High Street . . .'

It wasn't any use. I could see that Ellen's face had already glazed over.

'Not to worry,' said Mum. 'Tomorrow, Sam and Abi will wait for you.' She looked rather hard at me and Sam. 'Won't you?' she said.

We nodded. What else could we do?

'Just until she gets used to it,' said Mum.

# 3

'So what shall we do?' said Sam.

'Dunno,' I said. 'What'd you like to do?'

'Could go into town,' said Sam.

'Go and look at the shops?'

'Yeah! Go and look at the shops.'

It was Sunday morning and we were in the park, taking the dogs for their Sunday morning walk. Ellen was with us, and the Radish. They had both brought their yoyos and were competing with each other, seeing who could keep theirs going the longest. Ellen and the Radish got on really well. They both liked the same sort of games: yoyos and Snap and Snakes & Ladders.

'Only thing is,' I said, throwing a stick for Jack, 'I can't buy anything. I haven't got any money.'

'Me neither,' said Sam.

'I haven't got a bean.'

'I haven't got a bean. Doesn't matter! We'll just mosey around.'

Mosey was this new word she'd got. I don't know where she got it from, but me and Sam did a lot of moseying. We moseyed round the shops, we moseyed round the playground (when we weren't chucking netballs), we moseyed up the park.

'OK,' I said. 'Let's do that. Let's mosey!'

'What's mosey?' said Ellen.

'This is moseying.'

Sam went sauntering off across the park, rolling her shoulders and swaying her hips.

'See?' Sam swung round in a circle. 'It's what you do when you're going somewhere but not in a hurry.'

Of course, Ellen had to mosey too. She always had to do everything we did. She went clumping off trying to imitate Sam, humping her shoulders and jerking her hips, all splay-footed and stiff-legged. It would have been quite funny if it hadn't been so embarrassing. I mean, there were people in the park that *knew* us.

'Going to mosey with my yoyo,' said Ellen. 'Look! Here I go . . . mosey mosey yoyoyo! Mosey mosey—'

Once she'd got herself started, it was really difficult to stop her. Fortunately, Jack stopped her for us. I threw his stick, and he jumped up and caught it – and caught the yoyo, as well! Ellen screamed, 'Jack, that's my *yoyo!*' which naturally made Jack think it was some kind of game, so he at once goes streaming off across the grass, with Ellen lumbering after. I don't know why she couldn't run properly, but she couldn't. Maybe it was because her feet stuck out. It made her sort of . . . waddle. Like a penguin.

In the end, me and Sam had to round Jack up and wrestle with him before he'd let us have the yoyo back. It had a little row of teeth marks in it, which is something that would have made a lot of people really angry, but Ellen just giggled and said, 'Naughty boy! You've chewed my yoyo!'. She never got mad. Not with the dogs, not with anyone. Not even with that bad cat Felix when he jumped on the table and snitched her food. Even Sam had to agree that she was good-natured. Just embarrassing!

We took the dogs home and the Radish went off to potter in the garden while me and Sam went up to our room to change into our moseying gear. It was quite muddy in the park and you can't mosey round the shops in wellies and dirty old joggers.

When we got downstairs Mum said, 'Where are you two headed?'

'Just to the shopping centre,' said Sam.

'To mosey,' I said.

'Well, you make sure you mosey back here in time for dinner.'

We promised that we would. We were just

about to open the front door when Ellen appeared at the top of the stairs.

'Wait for me, wait for me!'

She came hurtling down – bang thump thud wallop! Everything shook when Ellen came down the stairs.

'What do you want?' said Sam.

I know it didn't sound very friendly, but we'd had to put up with Ellen all week. Well, ever since Tuesday, which was when she'd arrived. She tagged along to school with us, she came looking for us in the playground, she attached herself on the way home. She just wouldn't leave us alone!

'I'm coming to mosey,' she said. She had this big happy beam on her face. Sam and me looked at each other.

'I don't remember inviting you,' said Sam.

Ellen's face fell. I couldn't help feeling a bit sorry for her; but I desperately didn't want her with us! Sundays were *our* time, me and Sam's time. On Saturdays I went to my art classes and Sam did her gym, but Sundays were when we did things together. *On our own.* Without Ellen.

We set off down the path. I could hear Ellen breathing. She breathed really heavily, Like she had cotton wool stuffed up her nose. I still felt sorry for her. I suppose that was when I stopped and turned back. Which was a BIG MISTAKE.

She was standing there, all drooping, like a beaten puppy dog. I said, 'Sam—'

'We don't want her!' Sam hissed it, fiercely.

'I know,' I said, 'but—'

'No!'

It was then that Dad arrived on the scene. He took one look at Ellen and said, 'What's the matter, love?'

Two fat wobbly tears went plopping down Ellen's cheeks.

'They won't let me go and mosey!'

'Won't let you go and mosey?'

'No, and I've been practising! Look.' Ellen

clumped off along the path.

'Looks like a pretty good mosey to me,' said Dad. 'What's the objection to her going with you?'

We couldn't very well say that she was childish and embarrassing and we didn't want her to be with us. Not when she was standing right there. I mean, Sam is bold as brass and usually says just whatever pops into her mind, but not even Sam could have said a thing like that. It would have been really cruel.

'Well, see . . .' I stood on one leg and twisted the other round it. I don't know why I did that. I was, like, squirming. 'Cos I was trying to think of an excuse and I couldn't.

'We're just gonna mooch round the shops,' said Sam. 'Nothing exciting.'

'Well, but maybe Ellen would like to mooch, too.'

I felt like retorting, 'If we'd said we were

going to jump off a cliff she'd want to jump with us!' But of course I didn't.

'We're not *buying* anything,' said Sam.

'We haven't any money,' I said.

'No money? Well, let's see what we can do.' Dad dug his hand into his pocket. 'Here!' He held out three £1 coins. 'How about that? One for each of you. That should buy you a bag of crisps or something.'

What could we do? Sam made one last despairing attempt.

'Wouldn't you rather go and play with the Radish?'

'Don't want to play with the Radish.' Ellen was all beams again. 'Want to come with you!'

So there we were, stuck. We trailed down the road, with Ellen doing her usual hoppity-skippity act and me and Sam hanging behind, hoping people might think she was nothing to do with us. Sam was scowling. I knew that she held me to blame.

'If you'd just *come*, instead of hanging around—'

We might have got away before Dad turned up.

'Sorry,' I said.

'Too late now,' grumbled Sam. 'We'll just have to put up with it.'

When we went on our own Sam and me had ever such fun, moseying round the shops. What we did, we wandered round one of the big stores– like Hamlyn's, 'cos that was our favourite - looking at the clothes and the jewellery and picking out stuff we fancied. Then perhaps we might go to HMV to look at the records and the CDs, and then Smith's, for the magazines, and then the indoor market which sells just about everything. Sometimes we went to the Carpet Centre to see if they had any carpet squares going cheap (for the dolls' house), or the DIY, for wallpaper samples. It didn't matter if we couldn't buy anything; we enjoyed ourselves just looking. Browsing is what Mum calls it. (Dad calls it window-shopping and says it's a woman's thing.)

Well! We soon discovered that you couldn't just look with Ellen. You couldn't relax and browse. Wherever we went, she wanted to finger things. She kept picking stuff up and shouting, 'Hey, Abi! Want one of these? Sam, Sam, have one of these!'

If she wasn't touching, she was knocking things over. I mean, she didn't even *need* to touch. All she had to do was just breathe and things went toppling down. Like in the China & Glass department we were walking past this stand with really expensive glasses, all sparkly like diamonds. Ellen reached out a hand and said, 'Oh! Lovely glasses!' and before we realised what was happening the whole lot had gone bouncing on to the floor. Thank goodness it was soft carpet! 'Cos those glasses, they cost £45 each. Can you imagine it? £45? Just for a *glass*?

A woman came rushing over. She was really ratty. She told us to go away and stop touching at things.

'We weren't,' I said. I'd seen Ellen's hand. It hadn't even *reached* the glasses. 'We were just looking.'

'Well, don't!' snapped the woman. 'This is no place for children.'

We crept away with our tails between our legs. We felt really humiliated. Nothing like that had ever happened to us before! I thought it was a bit unfair, actually. We'd already told Ellen not to touch; we couldn't very well tell her not to *look*. Or to stop breathing. 'Cos I reckoned it was the breathing had done it. Breathing so heavily and creating a draft. They obviously couldn't stack their glasses very well if just a little bit of breathing could upset them.

We scurried away from China & Glass, keeping Ellen between us where she couldn't do any more damage, and went up the escalator to Young Fashions on the first floor. At least there wasn't anything there that she could break. To keep her quiet we said, 'Go and find an outfit for yourself. Something you'd really like.'

Guess what she chose? A little kiddy dress with puff sleeves and a sash. *Pink*. Bright pink! Sam shuddered.

'Ugh! How yucky can you get?'

'It's nice,' insisted Ellen. She took it off the rack and went lolloping over to a mirror, holding the dress up in front of her. Only she never got to look at herself 'cos halfway there she tripped over her own feet and went *flump!* on to the floor, with the dress all scrunched up beneath her. It was a nasty moment.

We shoved it back on the rack, ever so quickly before anyone could see it – I mean, it was OK, apart from a bit of a splat where one of Ellen's feet had trampled on it, but it wasn't too bad. I mean, it'd clean off easily enough.

It wasn't like she'd torn it or anything, so we didn't feel too guilty. But we didn't hang around. We got out *pronto* (as Dad would say).

On the way, Ellen bumped into a display stand and knocked a bunch of hats to the floor. She was worse than just embarrassing. She was a positive liability!

We left Hamlyn's and went to HMV to look at the records.

'Can I touch?' said Ellen.

'Yeah, but you gotta put things back,' said Sam.

So then she starts picking up CDs, one after another, and yelling, 'Abi, do you like The Pink Crystals? Sam, do you like Groove? Do you like Voice Over? Do you like Scream?' Shouting out the names of all these bands, really loud, for everyone to hear. Making a right exhibition of herself. And of us! People kept turning round and looking, and then old Ellen, she obviously thinks she's impressing them 'cos she starts on this pretend swooning and fainting when she finds one of her favourites. And by this time people are sniggering and Sam's gone bright red and I don't know where to put myself. I mean, we can't just walk out and leave her, but she is really overdoing it.

'Peter Kruger! Yum yum!' She's pressing the CD to her mouth and doing slobbery kissy noises over it. 'He makes me go all fffffffffffffff luttery, all fffffffffffff—'

'Stop it, will you! Just *stop* it!'

Sam, in a rage, snatches the CD from her, slams it back down and drags her out of the store. I follow, my face crimson.

'Where shall we go now?' says Ellen.

'I don't want to go anywhere!' snarls Sam.

Sam goes stalking off ahead of us, leaving me with Ellen.

'Hey, Sam! Sam!' I run to catch up with her. 'Let's go and have a Coke.'

'What about *her*?'

'Well . . .' I look at Ellen, doubtfully. She's picked a bit of gold foil from a cigarette pack out of a flower tub and is intently folding it into a little parcel. I wish we could just leave her, but I know that we can't. I heave a sigh. 'I guess she'll have to come with us.'

'If she comes with us, you keep an eye on her. Just make sure she doesn't do anything!'

Keeping an eye on Ellen was worse than keeping an eye on the Radish. Worse than keeping an eye on *Jack*. I made her sit with me while Sam went to get the Cokes.

'I'm enjoying myself,' she said. 'Are you enjoying yourself?'

I wasn't going to say yes, not when she'd gone and ruined it all, but I couldn't quite bring myself to say no.

'How's your mum?' I said.

'She's in hospital,' said Ellen.

'Yes,' I said. 'I know she is. You went to see her. Yesterday. Miss Davies took you.'

Miss Davies is the lady from Social Services.

'When's she coming home?'

'Dunno,' said Ellen.

'This week?'

'This week, next week . . .' Ellen was busy twisting the petals off an artificial fern she'd pulled out of a vase. 'This week, next week, some time, never. This week, n—'

'Soon,' I said. 'She *must* be coming home soon!'

It was really difficult trying to have a meaningful conversation with Ellen. Her mind flitted like a butterfly.

After we'd had our Cokes and crisps we wandered back out into the shopping precinct.

'What shall we do now?' Ellen wanted to know.

'Go home.' Sam said it grimly. She went marching off ahead again, leaving me to cope with Ellen.

Ellen plucked at my sleeve.

'Abi, I want to go to the loo!'

'SAM!' I bawled.

Sam stopped. 'What now?'

'Ellen wants to go to the loo!'

Sam muttered to herself. The Radish always wanted to go to the loo whenever we took him anywhere; but the Radish was only a little boy. He was only seven years old!

We went back up the escalator. There was a lovely loo in Hamlyn's, but we couldn't risk showing our faces in there again. Not with Ellen. She'd have to use the grotty old public one near the multi-storey car park.

Sam said. 'Can you manage by yourself? Or do you want us to come in with you?'

'I can manage,' said Ellen.

'Sure you won't get lost?' said Sam.

I kicked at her.

'We'll wait out here for you,' I told Ellen.

'And don't be all day,' added Sam.

We'd just settled down on the edge of a

flower tub – they're the right height for sitting on but a bit hard on the bum – when two girls from our school came by. A couple of Year 9s. I didn't know their names but I recognised their faces.

'See you got stuck with old Droopy Drawers,' said one.

They sniggered.

'Old Droopy Drawers Dredge!'

We watched, glumly, as they went sniggering on their way. I stuck my hands under my bum cheeks.

'It's only for another two weeks.' I felt that we had to try and look on the bright side. 'Her mum'll be home by then and things'll be back to normal.'

Sam just humped a shoulder and said, 'Huh!'

We waited for what seemed like ages for Ellen to come out of the loo. In the end Sam said, 'I've had enough of this!' and went storming in there. I heard her bellow,

'*Ellen*! It's time you were out!'

I thought that, being Ellen, she had most likely locked herself in and couldn't open the door. I had visions of the Fire Service having to come and batter it down. More embarrassment! But to my relief she appeared, dragged by Sam. She was giggling and looking sly.

'What have you been up to?' I said.

'Having a piddle!'

'*Ellen*!' I was shocked. Fancy saying a thing like that in public! 'What have you got there?'

She had a big bulge in the sleeve of her sweatshirt.

'What is it?' I said.

Ellen giggled again.

'Something!'

'What?'

With a look of great cunning, she slid a hand up her sleeve.

'*Loo paper?*'

A whole great wodge of it! Sheet after sheet, all folded over.

'What have you got that for?' I shrieked.

'Dunno,' said Ellen. 'Just fancied it. Want some?'

'You are completely batty,' said Sam. And then to me, 'We are *not* bringing her again!'

# 4

'I just don't see why she always has to *be* with us,' grumbled Sam.

It was the following Sunday and me and Sam were going shopping again. Real shopping, this time. We had money! Mum and Dad always gave us our pocket money once a fortnight, in the hope we'd learn how to plan ahead and not go rushing madly out to spend it all in one go. Which was what we usually did! When that happened, Mum stood firm.

'No more! If you've spent it, that's your problem. You'll just have to wait.'

Dad sometimes felt sorry for us and slipped us the odd pound (like he had last week) but woe betide him if Mum discovered!

'You're spoiling them,' she'd say. 'You're

defeating the whole object of the exercise. They'll never learn.'

But it was such fun, going round the shops with a purse full of money! At least, it was if we didn't have Ellen with us.

'I said we weren't taking her again,' said Sam.

'That's right.' I nodded. 'Not after last time.'

'Why can't she play with the Radish?'

'They could play Snap.'

'Yeah, or Snakes & Ladders.'

'Or just crawl around the floor.'

'Why can't she?'

We looked at each other.

'The Radish,' I said, 'is too old for that sort of thing.'

'Droopy Drawers isn't!'

We collapsed into giggles. It was awful, really, but we'd started calling her that. It sort of suited her. Everything about her drooped – including her knickers! We'd seen quite a lot of Ellen's knickers. She had this habit of coming into our bedroom, *totally* uninvited, not even bothering to knock, hurling herself on to one of the beds and sprawling about with her legs in the air. Jack and Daisy loved it! I mean, she was really good with the dogs. She let them lick her and jump on her and roll about with her. She didn't mind. But her knickers! They were a real embarrassment. All washed-out and baggy. I'd have been ashamed to be seen in them, but old Droopy, she didn't seem to care.

Mum came into the room while me and Sam were still giggling.

'Good!' she said. 'That's better.'

When she'd left us a few minutes ago, we'd both been in a right sulk. This was because Mum had caught us trying to sneak out of the house without Droopy.

Sam pulled her face back into a scowl. I did the same. We didn't want Mum thinking she'd got round us.

'Ellen's upstairs, crying,' said Mum. She paused, to let this sink in. 'She thinks you don't want her.'

Sam and me shuffled our feet.

'She's really embarrassing,' I said.

'And you can't manage to rise above it? Are you really both so insecure?'

'People laugh.' Sam said it defiantly.

'Yes, they do,' I said. 'They point and they laugh.'

'At you? Or at poor little Ellen?'

Little? Ellen wasn't little! She was a great lumping thing.

'Look,' said Mum, 'I can't force you to take her with you. I know how you feel and I can understand it. You're at that sort of age. You–'

Sam said, 'What sort of age?'

'An age,' said Mum, kindly, 'when your self-image is quite fragile.'

I blinked. What on earth was Mum talking about?

'We just don't want her messing things up,' said Sam.

'Oh, Sam, she wouldn't! I'm sure she wouldn't! She's got her pocket money to spend. It would make her so happy!'

'But, Mum, she's so childish,' I wailed.

'It's only one more week,' pleaded Mum. 'She'll be going home next weekend.'

There was a silence. I hooked my top teeth over my bottom lip and stared fixedly at the floor. I wasn't going to be the first to say anything. I'd got the blame last week!

Mum sighed.

'Perhaps I'm not being fair. I'll tell her you're meeting friends.'

'She'll only want to know why she can't meet them as well,' muttered Sam.

'She just wants to come *everywhere* and do *everything*,' I said.

'Even in the playground!'

'*Our* playground.'

'She ruins all our games. People think she's loopy.'

'She just won't listen! You can tell her over and over, go *away*, leave us *alone*—'

'I know, I know!' Mum held up a hand. 'Don't worry. I shouldn't have asked you. You go off and enjoy yourselves, I'll see to Ellen.'

Mum opened the door. 'Go on! Off you go. Quickly!'

Sam and me went through to the hall. Out of the corner of my eye I glimpsed a white shape, floating, at the head of the stairs. I knew that it was Ellen's big moon face. I knew that if I looked, it would be all pathetic and droopy. So I didn't look. I marched determinedly to the front door. And then I heard Sam yell, '*All right*, you can *come*! But only if you do as you're told!'

I spun round, my mouth gaping open. Sam humped a shoulder. This time, she would be the one to blame!

Old Droopy comes galloping down the

stairs quick as may be, before we can change our minds. She's all happy and beaming. She's wearing these really horrible clothes. Nerdy old anorak, baggy skirt, *ankle* socks and disgusting trainers with trailing laces. Yuck! But Mum's smiling at us.

'Have fun!' she says.

We set off down the road.

'This time, you gotta behave yourself.' Sam said it sternly. ''Cos this isn't just moseying, this is serious. We're gonna *buy* things.'

'I'm gonna buy things, too,' said Ellen.

'Where's your money?' I said. I was scared she'd have it somewhere daft, like in a pocket with a hole in it, but very proudly she pulled up her anorak to show me.

'Got it here!'

She had a rucksack. It was all hoicked up and made her look like she had this big hump growing out of her back, but at least it was safe. You had to think of these things, when you were with Ellen.

'What we gonna buy, what we gonna buy?' She started jumping up and down the minute we hit Hamlyn's. 'What we gonna buy, what we gonna—'

'*We're* gonna buy make-up,' said Sam. 'But it's a secret, see?' She thrust her face into Ellen's. 'You're not to go telling Mum.'

'Or Dad,' I added.

'Or Dad,' said Sam. 'Or the Radish.'

'Or the dogs.'

'Or Felix.'

'Not *anyone*. Right?' I tried to sound as stern as Sam had.

'Right.' Ellen nodded. 'Right, right! Not tell anyone. Not tell Mum. Not tell Dad. Not tell Radish. Not—'

Sam rolled her eyes.

'*Quiet.*' I put a finger to my lips. 'Someone might hear you.'

'Someone might hear me.' Ellen whispered it, bug-eyed. '*Quiet.*'

We set off through Menswear towards the Make-up department. We could hear old Droopy earnestly whispering to herself.

'Not tell Mum. Not tell Dad. Not tell Radish. Not tell dogs. Not tell Felix. Not tell *anyone*. Not tell Mum. Not tell Dad . . .'

At least it kept her quiet! Sort of. I mean, it was better than jumping and shouting.

The reason we didn't want Mum and Dad to know what we were spending our money on was 'cos we thought they might laugh at us. Once when I was about six I told them I wanted a 'peek-a-boob bikini' and they laughed and laughed. I still don't know what at. It was something I'd seen in a shop and I really fancied it. I hate it when people laugh at you!

But there was another reason, as well, and that was that Mum is quite old-fashioned. She's not specially strict or anything, but she doesn't approve of people our age wearing make-up or designer clothes or stuff like that.

I knew she'd say we were too young. But you've got to start somewhere. We'd be eleven before we knew it! What we were going to do, we were going to rush home and practise in secret in our bedroom. (My bedroom. Which in spite of her promise, Sam was already turning into a pigsty.)

'What shall we buy?' said Ellen. Her hand reached out towards a rack of lipsticks.

'Not them,' said Sam. She yanked Ellen away. 'That's fancy stuff, that is. That's expensive. Anything with a French name, like—'

'Dior,' I said. I knew about Dior. Dad had given Mum some Dior perfume for her birthday. It had cost the *earth*!

'See, we're experimenting,' said Sam. 'Got to find out what suits us. No sense paying a fortune.'

The cheaper brands were all along the back wall. Sam wanted some orange lipstick and silver nail varnish. I wanted some eyeshadow.

Blue eyeshadow. And some pink stuff to put on my cheeks.

'We can swop,' said Sam, 'and try each other's.'

We were so busy choosing things that we forgot about Ellen. We bought two lipsticks – Apricot for Sam and Mango for me; blue and brown eyeshadow; pink stuff for cheeks; a black pencil for doing eyes; and three lots of nail varnish – silver for Sam, gold for me, and a bright green one that we couldn't resist.

'We could use them all at the same time!' said Sam, excitedly.

'One on top of another?'

'No! Different colour for each nail.'

'In that case we ought to have five,' I said.

So we immediately rushed back and bought two more! I chose Mulberry and Sam chose Plum. We reckoned they'd look really good.

It wasn't till we went to pay for them that we remembered Ellen.

'Where is she?' I shrieked.

We thought we'd lost her! And then we saw her. Standing in front of a mirror, daubing at herself with purple lipstick.

'*Ellen!*'

She turned, beaming. I gulped. Sam said, 'Cripes!'

While me and Sam had been carefully selecting the colours we thought would suit us, old Droopy had gone round trying out all the testers. She was *plastered*. She'd done thick black rings round her eyes, like panda eyes. She'd spread sparkly green eyeshadow over one eyelid and glittery gold over the other. Her eyebrows had turned into big furry caterpillars crawling across her forehead; her cheeks were bright red, like apples; her lips like two wriggly worms, deep purple. Yeeurgh!

'You've made a right mess of yourself,' said Sam. 'A *right* mess.'

'Pretty,' said Ellen. She turned back to the

mirror. The wriggly worms spread themselves into a simper.

I giggled.

'It's not funny,' said Sam.

I thought it was! I thought it was hilarious. So did Ellen. She kept pulling her lips into all these different shapes, hoops and prunes and trumpets, and I kept giggling, I just couldn't help it, even though I knew it was getting Sam mad.

'We can't take her home like that!' she fumed.

We tried to make her scrub it off, but she wouldn't. She kept saying 'Pretty! Pretty!' and doing these little twirls and simpering at herself in every mirror that we passed.

'It *is* pretty,' I said. Sam glared at me. 'Well, it is!' I said; and then I went and ruined it by giggling again.

As we left the shopping centre we passed a group of girls that I recognised as Year 9s. Two of them were the ones we'd bumped into last week; the ones who'd sniggered and called Ellen 'Droopy Drawers'. They sniggered again when they saw what she'd done to herself.

'Hey, Droopy! Like the new face!'

Just for a second Ellen faltered; then she looked at me and Sam and said, 'Pretty!'

'It is,' I said. 'It's lovely!'

We could hear the Year 9s still sniggering. I gritted my teeth and told myself that it was Ellen's make-up they were sniggering at, not me. I was secure! I could rise above it. And anyway, she'd be going home next weekend. Another five days and we'd be back to normal! I wasn't going to let a little thing like this upset me.

Oh, but there was worse to come! Far worse. I just die even now when I think about it.

We were walking along the High Street. Most of the shops in the High Street are closed on a Sunday, so there weren't that many people about; but there were simply *hundreds* of cars. Hundreds and hundreds, all queued up waiting for the lights to change. And that was when it happened. This ghastly unspeakable thing. *Ellen's knickers fell down.* Her terribly baggy washed-out knickers. I didn't know where to look! I don't think Sam did, either. I mean, it was just *so* embarrassing.

Old Droops, she wasn't embarrassed. Guess what she did? Ever so calmly, she just stepped out of them and picked them up. And all those *thousands* of people watching, through their car windows!

'*Ellen!*' I said, horrified.

'What?' She giggled. 'I've lost my knickers!' She waved them at us, like a flag.

'Don't do that!' I shrieked. 'Everyone's watching you!'

'All right.' Ellen obligingly stopped waving her knickers. Instead, she scrunched them up and put them in her pocket. In her *pocket*! She beamed at me with her purple lips. She seemed to think that putting the knickers in her pocket made everything all right. I was scandalised.

'You can't walk home without knickers!'

'Why not?' said Ellen.

''Cos it's rude!'

'Yes, it is.' Sam suddenly sprang into life. 'It is! It's rude. Someone could look up your skirt.'

Ellen giggled again. '*That'd* be rude!'

Sam and me were at a loss. If we'd been in the shopping centre we'd have marched her up to the Ladies and made her get back into them. We'd have tied them round the middle, or pinned them, or something. But there wasn't a loo anywhere near! We had to walk back home with Ellen carrying her knickers in her pocket.

'Walk in front of us,' ordered Sam. 'That way, nobody can look up you.'

She couldn't even *walk* sensibly. She kept doing these little hops and skips, on and off the kerb. Me and Sam were in agony in case the wind suddenly blew her skirt up. I mean . . . walking around without any knickers!

'If she wasn't going home next weekend,' said Sam, 'I don't think I could bear it.'

'Another five days,' I said. 'I'm going to cross them off on the calendar.' Little did we know that our trials weren't yet over . . . We got home and wailed at Mum.

'Mum, she lost her knickers!'

'She walked home without any!'

'Mum, it was horrible!'

'When's she going home, Mum? Is it Friday? Please say it's Friday!'

That's when Mum hit us with it, zap, pow! The worst news of the week. Well, first of all she goes on about Ellen's mum not having much money and that's why she has to wear these baggy old washed-out knickers and how it must have been even more embarrassing for her than it was for us (it definitely was *not*). Then she says how she's going to go out first thing Monday morning and buy her some new ones from Marks & Spencer's.

'It's not fair on the poor child. I can't have people laughing at her.'

Then she hits us with it.

Ellen won't be going home this weekend after all.

'Her mum rang up while you were out. They're sending her off to a convalescent home for a few days. So . . . it looks like it'll be the weekend after.'

Sam went rushing into the garden to hurl a ball for the dogs. I trailed dismally upstairs to my bedroom. Another twelve days of Droopy! Another twelve days of Sam turning my room into a pigsty.

I felt thoroughly disgruntled.

# 5

'You promised!' I shrieked. I picked up a pair of Sam's shoes and hurled them across the bedroom. 'You promised you'd keep the place tidy!'

'I said I'd *try*. I didn't promise. I just said I'd *try*!'

'Well, then, why don't you?'

Me and Sam faced each other across the acres of bed which now seemed to take up almost all my bedroom. What wasn't taken up by bed was taken up by Sam's rubbish. Oceans of it, all cluttering the place up. Clothes on the floor, clothes on the beds, clothes on the chair. Shoes everywhere. Pair of tatty old jeans draped over the dressing table mirror. Horrible old hairbrush full of hair. Muddy trainers on the windowsill. Netball shorts hanging off the wardrobe door.

She'd even had the nerve to dump a load of stuff on top of my dolls' house! It was that that really got me. She knew how I felt about my dolls' house. It wasn't just a childhood toy that I'd stopped playing with when I was about nine. It was like it was ... well! My life's work. Some people devote themselves to collecting things. Stamps and things. Phone cards. China ornaments. *I* like to decorate my dolls' house. I like to lie in bed and look at it. And now I couldn't even see it because it was all covered in Sam's junk.

'You haven't even *bothered* to try!'

'Yes, I have,' said Sam.

'You haven't! You just *dump* things. You're so selfish!' I tore over to my dolls' house, clawed up all the tatty bits and pieces she'd parked there, and crammed them viciously into the wastepaper basket.

'Hey, stop that!' Sam galloped across the room, seized the basket and up-ended it on to the floor. All her rubbish came spilling back out, along with a horrid mess of empty Coke cans, dirty tissues (from our make-up session), old brown apple cores, withering banana skins, manky orange peel. *Ugh!*

'This is my good top!' bawled Sam. 'Look what you've done! You've gone and scrunched it up!'

'It's your own fault. Why can't you put things away after you?'

''Cos I don't want to put them away!'

'In that case' – huffing with fury, I tore round the bedroom snatching up armfuls of clothing as I went – 'they'll *all* get put in the bin!'

'You'd better not!' screeched Sam, and she grabbed at the waste basket and held it above her head where I couldn't get at it (Sam being loads taller than me).

I was so furious! You'll never guess what I did . . . I ran across the room and stuffed Sam's clothes up the chimney. That would teach her!

'You *dingbat*!' bellowed Sam. Dingbat was one of her words. I didn't know what it was supposed to mean, but it probably wasn't anything very nice.

She put an arm up the chimney and yanked at the trailing sleeve of her school blouse. The blouse, her school skirt and her school sweater came flumping out of the chimney. A shower of soot came out with them.

'Look at the mess you've made!'

I was a bit taken aback, to tell you the truth. We'd never had chimneys before we came to live in Auntie Marge's house. I hadn't realised quite how black and sooty they were.

'I'm not cleaning it up!' Sam was busy shaking her skirt. Thick black dust flew everywhere. 'You can do it!'

'I'm not doing it!' I was indignant. What cheek! 'If you could just try behaving like a normal civilised human being for once, it wouldn't have happened.'

'I *am* a normal civilised human being!'

roared Sam, battering at her skirt and raising clouds more dust. 'You're just a little niminy piminy creepy crawly' – she wriggled her fingers at me – 'pathetic pea-brained *pinhead!*'

'And you've got no manners,' I shouted. 'Moving into another person's bedroom and turning it into a tip!'

'Fuss fuss fuss! *Ning ning ning!* You're just so small-minded it's pathetic!'

Sam and me had never had such a row before. We'd never properly had a row at all. We were best mates. We were the superglue kids! But she just got me *so mad*. I felt like bashing her. I felt like throttling her. I felt like throwing something at her.

So I did. I snatched her hairbrush off the dressing table and hurled it straight at her.

I didn't really mean to hit her with it; it's just that I was in such a rage.

Sam gave a yell.

'I'll get you for that!'

She launched herself at me. Panting and

pumelling, we collapsed in a heap on one of the beds. I was yanking at Sam's hair. Sam seemed to be trying to stick her fingers up my nose. We didn't realise the Radish was standing in the doorway. Not until he gave a little whimper of distress, which brought us both to our senses.

'Radish!'

He must have heard us bawling and bellowing and come to investigate. He was standing in the doorway, his thumb in his mouth, his eyes all big and owly. I felt terrible, and I think Sam probably did, too. You can't fight in front of the Radish. He hates rows and loud voices. He was quite badly knocked about by one of his mum's boyfriends before he was taken into care, and it's left a legacy. That's what Mum says. Even if Dad, for instance, just trips over Felix (which he does quite often) and cries, 'Drat that animal! I'll have its guts for garters!' the Radish starts to shake. Well, he's getting a bit better now he's learnt that Dad doesn't really mean it, but he is still quite easily frightened.

'Radish, I'm sorry!' I ran over to him and put my arms round him. 'We weren't really fighting. It was only pretend! Wasn't it?' I turned and pulled a fierce face at Sam.

'Yeah. It's a new kind of game,' said Sam. 'War game!' She cackled.

'There's nothing to be scared of,' I said. 'Jack and Daisy aren't.'

At that moment, Jack and Daisy came crawling out from behind the dressing table. Jack took one look at me and Sam, and bolted downstairs. Daisy rolled over on to her back with her paws in the air. It's her 'please don't beat me' position. It's what she does if a big fierce dog comes up to her.

'Silly animals!' I said. I gave a little laugh. 'They thought we were serious! But we were just having fun.'

'Ha ha,' said Sam. 'Some fun!' She stalked past us, along the passage. 'I'm going to the bathroom. I'm going to *sponge* my school *uniform*.'

I knelt down and tickled Daisy's tummy. I felt bad about upsetting the dogs. Almost as bad as I felt about upsetting the Radish. I mean, they're only little innocent animals.

'Poor Daisy!' I crooned.

'Daithy come wiv *me*,' said the Radish. He tugged at her collar. 'Daithy come!'

Daisy didn't need any tugging. She scampered off downstairs with the Radish as fast as she could go. She was just glad to get away from the horrible shouting people.

I closed the bedroom door and slowly got into my school clothes. The bedroom looked in a worse state than ever. But *I* wasn't going to clean it up! I reckoned it was down to Sam.

All through breakfast we sat and glowered at each other. Sam's uniform had damp patches all over it and one sleeve of her blouse was a kind of muddy grey, but Mum was too busy to notice. She just about noticed me and Sam not speaking to each other.

'What's the matter with you two?' she said. And then, 'Well, whatever it is, you'll have to sort it out between yourselves. I haven't got time.'

She and Nan were going up to town together. To London, to the West End. They were catching an early train and spending the day looking round the shops. They were dead excited about it. Mum didn't want to know about me and Sam not being on speaking terms.

'Off you go!' she said, pushing us all out of the front door, me and Sam, the Radish and Droopy. 'I'll see you later.'

'Have a nice day,' said Sam.

'Thank you,' said Mum. 'We will!'

I hated Sam for saying that! Why hadn't I thought of it? Of course old Droopy had to go and pick up on it.

'Have a nice day, have a nice day.'

Over and over, like a parrot. Except with parrots it's quite funny and sweet when they repeat things. With Droopy it was just maddening. Also, with a parrot you could throw a cloth over its cage to keep it quiet. (Not that I ever would 'cos I think it would be unkind. I wouldn't ever keep a parrot in a cage to begin with.)

'Have a nice day, have a nice day.'

I wondered what Droopy would do if I took off my coat and smothered her with it. Would it shut her up? Or would she just go on wittering?

'Have a nice day, have a nice—'

Sam suddenly spun round.

'Be quiet!' she said. 'Just *be quiet!*'

Ellen blinked. I felt the Radish's hand steal into mine.

'. . . nice day,' whispered Ellen. 'Have a nice day.'

Sam made a strangulated noise, sort of halfway between a squawk and a gurgle, and went marching on ahead. She has these very long legs and also she's very athletic, so quite soon she had left us way behind. I was stuck with Droopy, doing her usual hoppity-skip on and off the kerb.

'Dance with me, Abi! Have a nice day!' She twirled about on the pavement, grabbing my arm and trying to make me join in. 'Dance, dance! Have a nice day!'

Inside my head I was going, *Stop it, stop it, stop it*! Even the Radish was looking at her as if she was loopy.

'Ellen, *please*,' I begged. 'You're making a spectacle of yourself.'

We got to school at last. Well, first we got to the Infants, where we said goodbye to the Radish.

'Bye-bye,' I said. I waved a hand. 'Be good!'

'Bye-bye,' said Ellen. 'Be good!'

And then quite suddenly, without any warning, she swooped on him and smacked a big wet kiss on his cheek. In front of all his little friends! I felt so embarrassed for him. I could see that the Radish was embarrassed, too. I mean, he was seven, for goodness' sake! He didn't want people to see him being slobbered over. He wanted to play the tough guy! All big and butch and swaggering.

'Bye-bye, Radish!' Now she was *blowing* kisses at him, through the gate. 'Byeee! Byeee!'

Some little kids on their way in started sniggering. I saw the Radish's cheeks fire up and I felt really sorry for him.

'See, he doesn't like you doing that,' I told Droopy, as we walked up the road. 'He's got his image to think of.'

She nodded. 'Right! Right! Got his image to think of.'

And then, you'll never believe it, she goes and smacks a big wet kiss on *me*. I'm still reeling from the shock when she goes lolloping off towards the Senior school, flapping her hand and crying, 'See you, Abi! Have a nice day!'

Mary-Jo Mitchell was standing nearby. She's the sort of girl who always manages to be around when something embarrassing happens. She curled her lip in a superior smile.

'Old Droopy Drawers got a crush on you, or something?'

Now it would go right round the class . . .

All day in school, me and Sam avoided each other. We'd had little tiny tiffs in the past, but never anything like this. I tried reminding myself that we were the superglue kids. We didn't have rows! We weren't like other people. But I was just still too mad at her. And she was obviously still mad at me.

Everybody noticed that we weren't sitting together.

'Have you fallen out?' said Lauren Babcock. Lauren Babcock and her friend Alison Peach are two people that we *particularly* despise.

'None of your business!' I said, haughtily.

'Well, pardon me for breathing,' said Lauren.

She's always coming out with these dumb remarks.

'We were only trying to be friendly,' said Alison.

Only trying to be *nosey*.

'It's still none of your business!'

I don't usually snap, but I couldn't think of anything else to say. I mean, I wasn't letting on that me and Sam had had the biggest row of all time. Not to those two. They'd only gloat; they were gloating sort of people.

After lunch, in the playground, Sam played netball with Mary-Jo and Lissie and one or two others. I could have joined in; I mean there was nothing to stop me, but I knew they didn't really want me to. They were happier on their own, without me always dropping the ball or tripping over my feet or doing something stupid. Not that I was as bad as Droopy; she was completely useless. But I'm one of those people, I always get picked last when it comes to teams. And anyway, I hated Sam so much I didn't want anything more to do with her. I didn't want to be anywhere near her. She'd turned my bedroom into a tip and I would never forgive her for it. *Ever.*

So I mooched round the playground on my own, frowning and staring into space, trying to make like I was solving problems or was lost in deepest thought. In fact all I was thinking was, *I hate her, I hate her! I wish she'd never come to us!*

While I was mooching I saw Droopy appear at the gates and I immediately ran behind a tree and hid. By peering round the trunk, I could just see her. I watched as she came into the playground. Her head turned this way and that. She was looking for me. She could see Sam and the others playing netball, but it was me she wanted. She wasn't too sure of Sam. Sam yelled at her. Sam was mean. Mean and selfish and a loud-mouthed bully. Unlike me. A little halo twinkled over my head as I hid behind the tree trunk. I wasn't mean and selfish and loud-mouthed! I was kind and gentle and patient. And I was tidy. I didn't go round messing people's bedrooms up.

I peeped out again to see what Droopy was doing. She'd given up looking for me and had gone clumping into the middle of the netball players. And oh, boy, they were getting really mad! I could see Sam starting to simmer. I could always tell when she was about to blow. She had this habit of clenching her fists and pulling this horrible face, with her lips all curled back and her teeth bared like a wild animal's.

She *was* like a wild animal. It's true I'd hit her on the head with her hairbrush, but I hadn't meant to. She didn't have to hurl herself at me.

Now she was doing it to old Droopy. Running at her. Shouting.

'*Go away! Just go away and leave us alone!*'

I watched as poor old Droops went lumbering off, all splay-footed, in a panic. I felt kind of sorry for her, but not quite sorry enough to come out from behind my tree. I didn't want to get stuck with her.

Instead I got stuck with this girl Jasmine Potter that has a drippy nose. I know it's not her fault, but it drips all the time and I just didn't see why she couldn't blow it occasionally instead of sniffing. Me and Jasmine had hung out together, just a little bit, when I first started at Larkhall. (That is the name of our school.) But that was before Sam came. After Sam came, we sort of drifted apart. Not that we'd ever been best friends, or anything. Not even friends at all, really. But Jasmine has always had it in for Sam. She reckons it was Sam's fault we didn't hang out any more.

Anyway, she comes up to me in afternoon break, with this big goofy smile on her face, and goes, 'Now you and Sam aren't together any more, do you want to be friends with me again?'

I don't! I really, desperately, *don't*. But who else is there? By the time you reach Year 6, everyone's all paired off. It's only people like poor old drippy Jasmine who's still on her own. And now me. Drippy Jasmine and me.

'Well? D'you want to?' she says.

I mumble that I'll think about it.

'We could make a foursome,' says Jasmine.

I frown. 'Foursome with who?'

Jasmine beams.

'Alison and Laurie.'

Alison Peach and Lauren Babcock! My two *least* favourite people.

I tell Jasmine that I'll let her know, but she's almost as hard to shake off as Droopy. She sticks with me all round the playground.

I don't even like her!

She's not at all an inspiring sort of person. She doesn't like dogs, for one thing, and I can't stand people that don't like dogs.

The bell rings at last and we slowly walk back across the playground. Sam's laughing very loudly, like a hyena, at something Lissie Thomas has said. I pass within a centimetre of her but she just looks straight through me. So I link my arm in Jasmine's and stick my head in the air and make like Sam doesn't exist. I can't see that we'll ever be on speaking terms again.

# 6

That afternoon, I got back home before Sam. She had a netball practice, which I was really glad about 'cos I didn't want to walk home with her. Instead, I walked with the Radish.

And Droopy.

And Jasmine.

They both attached themselves to me as I left school. Drippy and Droopy. Only they couldn't just *walk*. Droops was doing her usual skippity-hop stuff, on and off the kerb. She tried to make the Radish join in, but he wouldn't. He said, 'Ellen, that'th *baby* thtuff!'

She still went on tugging at him. In the end I had to say, 'Ellen, stop it! He doesn't want to.'

So then she tries it on with Jasmine, and you'll just never believe it but Jasmine thinks it's *fun*. Next thing I know they're both at it, holding hands and skippity-hopping like mad things. The Radish looks at me, anxiously. I say, 'Let's pretend we don't know them,' and me and the Radish walk on ahead, very dignified, with our noses in the air.

I feel really sorry for the poor little Radish. He was such a nerdy, weedy, scaredy little thing when he first came to us. It took him such a long time to start getting brave. And now old Droopy's going and making him look ridiculous in front of all his mates!

She's making me look ridiculous, too. A couple of boys from my class are on the other side of the road. Gary Copestake and Charlie Potts. They're bullies at the best of times. Sam's about the only girl they're scared of, and Sam's not with us!

As me and the Radish walk past, with the Goon Sisters doing their double act behind us, the two boys start blowing rude noises at us and shouting things – stupid things which

I'm not even going to bother writing down. Then Gary starts clumping on and off the kerb, imitating Ellen, and Charlie Potts yells something that sounds like 'Wey hey!' and makes like he's pulling his knickers down. And then they both start chanting: 'Droopy Drawers lost her drawers! Poor old Droopy lost her drawers!'

I go all hot and prickly. How do they know? Who's told them? I glance back at Ellen, to see how she's taking it. It's stopped Jasmine in her tracks, 'cos Jasmine knows what those boys are like; but Droopy's beaming all over her face. She thinks they're just being friendly! She's actually *waving* at them . . .

I can't wait to get home!

We left Jasmine at the corner of the High Street. For a minute I thought Droopy was going to go with her, and for a minute I was almost tempted to let her, but then I thought of what Mum would say.

'Oh, Abi, how could you? You know she

needs someone to keep an eye on her!'

So I yelled 'Oi!' and yanked at her arm. 'This way!'

'I'm coming, I'm coming!' Skippity-hop. 'Going to have *tea*!' She biffed the Radish on the head with her school bag. 'Tea for me!' Biff. 'Tea for you!' Biff. 'Tea for—'

'Ellen, *stop* it,' I said.

The Radish was fingering his head and looking as if he might burst into tears. She'd biffed him really hard.

'You hurt him,' I told her.

That was a mistake. She immediately swooped on him, going 'Sorry, sorry! Make it better! *Mwah*!' Big slurping kiss on top of his head.

'Ellen!' I screeched.

The Radish shook himself, like the dogs do when they get wet. Droopy swooped again, but this time the Radish was too quick for her. He darted into the road – right in the path of a passing car. I just managed to grab him before he was mown down. 'Will you *please* behave yourself?' I said to Ellen. 'I have had enough.' It was what Mum always said to me and Sam. I said it again. 'I have had *enough*.'

I seized the Radish's hand, gave Ellen a shove, and marched them both very firmly up the road. By the time we finally got home I was in an even worse temper than I'd been before. Why was it always me that got lumbered with Droopy? Sam never took her fair share! Just like she never put her things away after her. *Was I expected to do everything?*

Mum and Nan were back from their shopping expedition and all full of the things they had seen and done.

'Oh, it was lovely!' said Nan. 'Just so nice to see a bit of life.'

'We went up Oxford Street,' said Mum. 'Very crowded.'

'Very crowded.' Nan nodded.

'But the shops!'

'Oh! The shops!' said Nan.

'You'd have had a wonderful time, Abi.'

Instead of which, I thought, I'd had a perfectly horrible time, what with Sam, and then Jasmine, and then Droopy.

Droopy began chanting that *she* would have had a wonderful time, too.

'I would have had a wonderful time, I would have had a wonderful time, I would have—'

Mum hastily agreed that of course she would.

'Maybe one day your mum will take you up there. And maybe one day,' said Mum, turning to me, 'I'll take you and Sam.'

'And me!' said Droopy, jumping up and down. 'And me, and me!'

'You won't be here,' I said.

Her face fell. 'Why won't I?'

' 'Cos you'll be back in your own home.' And good riddance! I was in a right mean mood.

'Well!' said Mum. 'And what kind of day have you had?'

Droopy clapped her hands. 'Lovely, lovely!'

Droopy never got mean moods. She was always happy. It didn't matter how horrid you were to her, she was always bright and bubbly and cheerful.

'Abi?' said Mum. 'How about you? Have you had a nice day?'

Grumpily I said, 'No.'

'Oh, What a little ray of sunshine,' said Nan.

It really makes me curl up when Nan says things like that. I glared at her across the kitchen.

'My, my! If looks could kill,' she said.

'Why such a crosspatch?' said Mum. 'What was wrong with your day?'

'Everything.' I scowled.

'Want to tell me about it?'

I humped a shoulder. 'Not particularly.' I knew she wouldn't be sympathetic. If I told her about Sam messing my bedroom up or Droopy embarrassing me, she'd only remind me yet again that it was 'just for a short time'. And if I told her about drippy Jasmine, she'd read me a lecture about how Jasmine couldn't help being drippy and I ought to learn to be a bit more tolerant.

Well! I wasn't feeling tolerant. I was feeling sour.

'Hmm!' said Mum. 'Well, I'm glad to say that Nan and I had a lovely day, and thank you very much for asking. Now, while I get some tea I wonder if you'd mind just taking the vacuum cleaner and a duster up to your bedroom.'

'What for?' I said.

'I see a load of soot has come down the chimney. It's made a terrible mess! I haven't had a chance to clear it up; we only got in half an hour ago. So I wonder if you'd very kindly mind doing it for me?'

'No.' I stuck out my lower lip, which is this

thing I do when I'm feeling extra-specially stubborn.

'*No?*' said Mum.

'It's up to Sam! It's her fault!'

'You mean, Sam made soot fall down the chimney?'

'Yes! Well . . .' I hesitated. In fact it had been me that had made the soot come down by stuffing Sam's clothes up there. But it was still her fault!

I said this to Mum. 'She's the one to blame, not me! I don't see why I should have to clear it up. I always have to do everything round here. It's not fair! I d—'

'Oh, Abi, for goodness sake!' I could see that Mum was losing patience. 'I'm really not interested in any of this! I'm far too tired.'

*She* was tired? She'd been up in town, enjoying herself! I'd been at school, working.

'Just do as I ask you, there's a good girl! Take the vacuum cleaner and the duster and clear up the mess for me. *Please.*'

Mumbling and muttering to myself, I lugged the vacuum cleaner up the stairs. I was quite shocked when I opened my bedroom door. I'd forgotten what a state we'd left the place in! There was a huge great pile of soot on the carpet and horrid black dust all over the mantelpiece and the dressing table. Plus, of course, there were still Sam's clothes lying about everywhere. *And* the contents of the wastepaper basket.

In a sudden fury I tore back downstairs, snatched a black bin-bag from under the sink, galloped back up with it and began stuffing Sam's clothes in just as fast as I could go. Then I tied the handles in a knot, opened the window and with a great OOOF! I hurled the sack into the garden.

I felt a whole lot better when I'd done that. I dusted all the surfaces and vacuumed up the floor and put the contents of the wastepaper basket back where they had come from. I went downstairs in really quite a good mood. That would teach Sam to mess my bedroom up!

Sam came in while we were having tea. She pointedly ignored me.

'Did you have a nice day?' she said to Mum.

'Lovely,' said Mum. 'Did you?'

'Brilliant!' said Sam.

I didn't know what was supposed to be so brilliant about it. Wait till she saw what I'd done with her things!

What I thought would happen, I thought she'd go upstairs and think Mum had been there, tidying up after her. Then she'd start looking for some of her stuff and she wouldn't be able to find it. Ha!

Only it didn't happen quite like that. What happened, Sam went into the garden to play with the dogs and came roaring back in, in an absolute rage, carrying the black plastic sack and an armful of clothes.

'*Who did this?*'

There was only me and Mum in the

kitchen. Nan had gone upstairs for a lie-down, Droops and the Radish had gone into the other room to watch telly.

'Was it you?' She waved the sack in my face. It must have caught on something prickly on the way out of the window 'cos it was all in tatters and Sam's clothes were all soggy and muddy. The dogs had been out there, earlier. They'd obviously trampled on them.

'You wait!' yelled Sam.

Mum watched in bewilderment as first Sam, and then me, went charging out of the kitchen. Sam took the stairs three at a time and reached the bedroom well ahead of me. As I burst through the door, she was in the act of emptying a drawer full of jumpers out of the window. My jumpers. I screamed, and ran at her.

'What are you girls up to?' thundered Mum, from the doorway.

'It's her fault!'

I pointed at Sam. Sam pointed at me.

'She did it first!'

We both spoke at the same time.

'She chucked my clothes out the window!'

'She doesn't even try!'

'What are you talking about?' said Mum.

'Mum, she's so messy!'

'*She's* just a dingbat!'

'*She's* just a—'

'Stop this! The pair of you!' Mum thumped angrily with her fist on the bedroom door. 'I've had a long day! I don't need any of this!'

'Whatever is all the shouting?' Now Nan, too, had appeared in the doorway. 'My goodness me, I thought someone was being murdered!'

'Someone still might be,' muttered Sam, and she looked at me with her eyes all malevolent and glittery.

'Selfish pig!' I shouted.

'Pinhead!'

'Dear, dear' said Nan. 'This sounds serious.'

'It sounds extremely childish to me,' said Mum. 'Let's have this out. *Sensibly.*' She shut the bedroom door. 'Sit down! Both of you.'

Sam and me stood there.

'I said, *SIT DOWN!*' roared Mum.

'Well, I certainly intend to,' said Nan.

Nan set herself down on my little wicker chair. Sam and me, still glowering at each other, parked ourselves on opposite sides of the bed, as far away from each other as possible.

'Right,' said Mum. 'Now let's have your grievances. Abi, you first!'

I poured it all out, about Sam being so slovenly, messing my room up, not even trying, refusing to put things away after her.

'She leaves them all over the place! It's horrible! She makes the room look like a tip.'

Sam sat there, simmering. She could hardly wait for it to be her turn!

'All right,' said Mum. 'We've heard Abi's

side. Now let's have Sam's.'

Sam sprang to her feet and began bouncing energetically on the bed like it was a trampoline, telling Mum how I was a self-righteous goody-goody prig and so small-minded it was unbelievable.

'I didn't want to share with her any more than she wanted to share with me! All she ever does is nag.'

I rose up, indignantly. 'I do not nag!'

'You do so!'

'I do not!'

'You—'

'Stop!' Mum held up a hand like a traffic policeman. 'I've heard both sides. I can't say I'm very impressed. I would have thought, just for a few weeks, you could have managed to get along together. I would have thought Sam might have made a bit more of an effort just as I would have thought Abi might have been a bit more tolerant. Instead you've behaved like a couple of spoilt brats.

I'm extremely disappointed! What is to be done?'

'I'll tell you what's to be done.' Nan struggled up out of her chair. 'If they can't share a room without quarrelling I shall obviously have to cut short my stay and go home.'

There was a silence.

'Well?' Mum looked grimly from Sam to me. 'Is that what you want? You want Nan to be driven out of the house?'

We hung our heads and muttered no.

'She makes all this effort, comes all this way to see us—'

'We don't want Nan to go home!' I said.

'No, we don't,' said Sam.

'So do you think,' said Mum, 'that you could possibly manage to get through the next few days without throwing each other's things out of the window?'

I giggled.

'Well? *Do* you?' said Mum.

'She stuffed my clothes up the chimney,' said Sam. And then she giggled, too, and before we knew it we were practically doubled over. It just suddenly seemed so silly . . . stuffing clothes up the chimney!

'Yes, well,' said Mum. 'I'm glad you can see the funny side of it.' She nodded at Nan. 'Let's leave them to it.'

Once Mum and Nan had gone, me and Sam came to our senses. We stopped giggling and sat looking at each other, very solemn and shamefaced.

'I didn't really mean all those things I said about you,' said Sam.

'Nor did I,' I said. 'I mean, what I said about you.'

'But it's true,' admitted Sam. 'I didn't really try.'

'Yes, but I expect I'm too used to being an only child,' I said. 'I never had to share before. I'm probably a bit too . . .' I tried to think of the right word. 'A bit too pernickety.'

'But we shouldn't have quarrelled.'

'No, we shouldn't.'

'I'll say sorry,' said Sam, 'if you will.'

'Let's do it together... one... two...
three, SORRY!' We both shouted it out at
the same time.

'It's her,' said Sam. She meant Droopy.
'Getting on our nerves.'

We both agreed that Droopy was
impossible. I know it was horrid of us, and
I'm really ashamed of it, but we had a long
finding-fault-with-Droopy session and it
made us feel better.

'We mustn't ever fight like that again,' I
said.

Sam agreed. 'We mustn't take things out
on each other.'

'So, who do we take them out on?' I
wondered. 'Other people?'

'Yeah! Take them out on other people.'

'You mean, like... Her Next Door and—'

'I know!' Sam giggled. 'We could make

wax dummies and stick pins in them!'

'That'd be fun!' I liked that idea. I enjoy making things. 'We'd need some modelling wax. We could go and get some Friday! Soon as we break up.'

'Yes,' said Sam, 'and we won't tell Droopy!'

# 7

The mini mart on the corner of our road didn't have any modelling wax or we'd have started in straight away making models. We had a whole long list of people we were going to make them of.

There was Gary Copestake and Charlie Potts (to pay them back for being bullies). There was Lauren Babcock, who'd swiped my best rubber and then pretended it was hers and refused to give it back to me. There was Mr Miah, one of our teachers, for telling Sam off for something that wasn't her fault. (Teachers are always doing that.) And there was Her Next Door, who'd complained again to Mum about Jack and Daisy. She'd said they barked when me and Sam got home from school. Well, of course they barked! They were excited. It was their way of saying hello. It only went on for a few minutes, so I don't know what her problem was. We were going to stick pins all over her.

*When* we could get some modelling wax!

Sam had said the one thing we mustn't ever do was take things out on each other, and I agreed. But that didn't mean we could take them out on poor old Droopy. I think we both felt kind of sorry for her, or at least we did when she wasn't being annoying. Which unfortunately was most of the time! She was just an extremely annoying sort of person. But we knew she couldn't help it. We knew we had to be patient with her. And we tried! We really, really did.

We kept reminding ourselves that she'd be going home at the end of the week. I was crossing the days off on my calendar! When Mum, all suspicious, asked me what I was doing it for, I told her it was the number of days to go till the end of term, which happened to be true. I'm not sure whether she believed me. She knew how me and Sam felt about having Droopy attaching herself to us everywhere we went. I think she probably guessed the real reason I was doing it 'cos she patted my hand, which isn't at all a Mum-like thing to do, and whispered, 'Proud of you! Both of you. Keep it up! Not long to go.'

I told Sam what Mum had said and Sam immediately looked guilty. She confessed that she had just been having horrid thoughts.

I said, 'What kind of horrid thoughts?' and Sam said, 'Really horrid.' She'd been thinking about breaktime and about Droopy coming into our playground and blundering, uninvited, into the middle of the netball game.

I said that if you were a mad-keen netball player then that was probably enough to make you have horrid thoughts; but Sam said, 'Not as horrid as the ones I was having.' So then I came over all noble and said that just for the next few days, if Sam liked, I would take

Droopy under my wing and walk round the playground with her so that the netball players could get on with their game.

'Abi!' cried Sam. 'Would you really?'

I swallowed. What had I let myself in for? But I said yes, I would really, and Sam gave a great screech and leapt up and punched the air and told me I wasn't a dweeb or a dork or a dingbat or any of the other things she'd thought about me while we weren't on speaking terms.

'You're ace!'

'Well, but we are best friends,' I said. It was what being friends was all about. Making sacrifices.

'I'll tell you what I'll do,' said Sam, generously. 'I'll stay with you all the way to school! Instead of going on ahead. How about that?'

I said that that would be nice. 'I get so embarrassed when she starts jumping about.'

'This way we'll both be embarrassed,' said

118

Sam. 'That's fair, isn't it?'

I agreed that it was. I mean, it would have been even nicer if Sam had said I could go on ahead, but at least both of us being embarrassed was better than just me being embarrassed on my own.

'And I won't have any more horrid thoughts,' vowed Sam.

'Me neither,' I said.

And so for the rest of the week we were as patient as could be. We all walked to school in a bunch, and when Droopy started on her hoppity-skip routine me and Sam didn't say a thing. We just looked at each other. At breaktime I kept my promise. As soon as Droopy appeared, peering anxiously this way and that, I left the netball game and went running over to her. Jasmine saw me, and she came running, too, so there I was, stuck with both of them. But every time a horrid thought tried creeping in, I quickly started thinking other thoughts and got rid of it.

'They are so mean,' gushed Jasmine, 'not letting you play with them.'

'Are you speaking to me?' I said.

'Yes, I think it's perfectly hateful of them. Just because they're good at netball and you're not. I know exactly how you feel,' said Jasmine.

Horrid thoughts started creeping up. I banished them immediately.

*Hey diddle diddle!* I sang in my head.

'I could play if I wanted,' I said.

Jasmine looked at me, pityingly, like she thought I was just making it up.

'I mean, you're probably good at loads of things they're not. They haven't any right to feel superior.'

*Hey diddle diddle! Tumty tumty tum.*

'I hate gamesy sort of people, don't you?' Jasmine linked her arm through mine. 'That Lissie Thomas and Mary-Jo think they're so wonderful!'

She didn't dare say anything bad about

Sam. She knew I wouldn't stand for it.

We put up with Droopy on the way to school, we put up with her on the way back from school. We put up with her bursting into our bedroom without even bothering to knock. We put up with her helping herself to our make-up that we'd bought and smearing it all over her face. We put up with her slopping and slurping at the meal table. As a rule we'd pull faces or make loud groaning noises, but we weren't doing that any more. We were telling ourselves that poor old Droopy couldn't help the way she was and in any case she was only going to be with us for another four days . . . three days . . . two days . . . one day . . .

On Thursday we broke up for the Easter holidays. Droopy's mum was coming to collect her the next day. We'd been hoping and praying it would be in the morning, but of course it wasn't. Miss Davies, who is the lady from Social Services, rang Mum to say they'd be round 'some time in the afternoon – about three-ish'.

'*Bother*,' said Sam. She didn't say it in front of Droopy. She waited till we were on our own. 'Bother, bother, BOTHER! Now she'll want to come into town with us.'

Me and Sam had planned on going in to buy our modelling wax.

'Could go in the afternoon,' I said.

'If Mum'd let us. Probably say we'd got to be here.'

Which was exactly what Mum did say.

'It would be terribly unkind if you weren't here to say goodbye. It's not much to ask, is it?'

'N-no.' I mumbled it at the carpet. 'S'pose not.'

'Well, of course it's not! Why can't you go shopping in the morning?'

'Wanted to go in the afternoon.'

'Why? For any special reason?'

'Dunno.' I humped a shoulder. 'Just did.'

'If you're worried about Ellen wanting to come with you—' I looked up, quickly. Mum laughed. 'Oh, so that's it, is it? And you couldn't bring yourself to tell me!'

'Thought you'd be cross,' I muttered.

'No, I'm not cross. You and Sam have been very good all week. Don't worry about Ellen, I'll see she stays here with me.'

Well! First thing after breakfast, Friday morning, we took the dogs for their walk. We always do this when we're on holiday. Mum says it's only fair as she has to do it during term time.

'What we gonna do when we get back?' said Droopy.

Sam and me shot these glances at each other.

'*You're* going to stay and pack,' I told her, ''cos your mum's coming for you this afternoon.'

'Or had you forgotten?' said Sam.

'Hadn't forgotten.'

'No,' I said, 'and I bet you haven't packed!'

'Have packed. Packed last night. All ready to go.' Droopy did a little twirl, *thump thump thump*, in a triumphant circle. 'Do what I like this morning!'

My heart sank.

'So what we gonna do? What we gonna do?'

I pulled a despairing face at Sam. Sam cleared her throat.

'We haven't yet decided.'

'Go shopping?'

'I *said*,' said Sam, 'that we haven't yet decided!'

As soon as we got home we shot upstairs, ripped off our walking clothes, threw on our moseying gear, and pelted back down. Horrors! Droopy was already there, waiting . . .

'Go shopping?'

I screeched, 'Mum!'

Mum was working on the computer, doing Dad's accounts. She came out into the hall.

'Now, Ellen,' she said, 'I think perhaps you ought to let the girls go by themselves this time. They have things to do – and so do you! I'm sure you haven't finished all your packing. Why don't you go upstairs and check that you haven't left anything out? We'll both go up, shall we?'

Mum shepherded Droopy up the stairs, making 'off you go' motions at me and Sam as she did so. We scuttled!

But old Droopy wasn't as daft as she sometimes appeared, 'cos next thing we know she's bawling, 'Sam! Abi!' and plopping up the road after us on her big splayed feet.

'Quick!'

Sam grabs me and we run. We tear along the High Street and dive into the first shop we come to, which happens to be a newsagent. Sam's going like the wind and she's dragging me with her. Old Droopy's left way behind. She'll never be able to find us!

I whisper, 'How did she get out?'

'Dunno,' says Sam. 'Let's hide!'

Me and Sam cram ourselves behind a rack of magazines at the far end of the shop.

'She must have given Mum the slip.'

'But how?'

All I could think was that Mum had taken her upstairs and left her in her room, then gone back down to get on with her work. And the minute her back was turned, old Droopy had scooted.

'Watch it!'

Sam prodded me. I looked out and saw Droopy plodding past the newsagent. Sam ducked down. I snatched up a magazine and held it open in front of my face. We stayed there, frozen like statues, until a voice said, 'Just what exactly do you kids think you're doing?'

Help! It was the man who owned the shop. He's very bad tempered. He hates children. He has a big notice sutck on his window:

ONLY TWO SCHOOL CHILDREN
ALLOWED IN AT A TIME.

'There's only two of us,' said Sam.

'I don't care how many of you there are, I
asked you what you were doing.'

'Reading this magazine,' I said, brightly. 'I
might buy it.'

'You'll do no such thing!' The magazine
was torn away from me, and me and Sam
found ourselves bundled outside. Fortunately
there was no sign of Droopy.

'I don't see what he had to do that for,' I
grumbled. 'Doesn't he *want* to sell things?'

Sam giggled. 'Did you see what you were
reading?'

'No.' I rubbed crossly at my elbow
where I had banged it as I was being hustled
out of the shop. 'What difference does it
make?'

'It was a rude one,' said Sam. She put her
face close to mine. 'Naked ladies!'

'Don't be disgusting,' I said.

'I'm not being! It was! You were looking at naked ladies!'

'I was not!'

'Looked like you were.'

'Well, I wasn't! And anyway, I don't believe you.'

We walked on, along the High Street.

'I wonder where Droopy's gone?' I said.

'What's it matter?' said Sam.

'Well . . .' I was beginning to have a bit of a conscience. 'So long as she's gone back home.'

'Dunno where else she'd go.'

I thought that, being Droopy, she could have gone almost anywhere; but as Sam pointed out, it wasn't our responsibility.

'She wasn't supposed to be with us.'

'I s'pose not.'

'Well, she wasn't! Just forget about her.'

'But she's so daft! She could walk under a bus, or . . . or anything!'

'Who cares?' said Sam. And then she

looked ashamed and muttered, 'She'll be all right.'

Two seconds later we turned into the shopping centre and there she was, old Droopy, with her thumb in her mouth, gazing vacantly into space. Sam groaned. I felt relieved that she hadn't been run over but I did most desperately wish we could sneak past without her noticing. Not a chance! She'd already seen us. Her face broke into this big happy beam.

'There you are!' she said. 'I wondered where you'd gone!'

I waited for Sam to snarl 'Get lost!' or 'Go away and leave us alone!' But Sam's one of those people, she blusters a lot and makes like she's really tough, but underneath she's quite a softie. She just doesn't like anyone to know.

Sternly, she said to Droopy that we were going to do some shopping, 'But you can't come with us. Not this time. You gotta stay here' – she pushed her down on to a bench – 'and wait for us.'

Droopy didn't want to sit and wait for us. She wanted to come with us!

'I won't touch anything,' she said. 'Promise!'

'That's not the point,' said Sam. 'You can't come with us 'cos' – I could see Sam's brain madly trying to think of a reason – ' 'cos we're gonna *buy* something. Like a . . . a present! See? So you stay there' – she gave Droopy a little shove – 'and we'll come and get you.'

'And whatever you do,' I said, '*don't move!*'

'That's right,' said Sam. 'You just wait.'

'We'll be back.'

'Yeah! We will. We'll be back.'

'With presents?'

'I told you,' said Sam, 'that's what we're gonna buy. Can't come with people when they're buying presents, can you?'

Droopy shook her head, but she didn't seem too certain.

'You won't move, will you?' I said. ''Cos we won't be very long.'

Me and Sam hurried off, leaving Droopy all forlorn on her bench. 'What did you say that about presents for?' I hissed.

'Well . . .' Sam squirmed. 'I dunno! Just seemed like a good idea.'

'But now she'll think we're going to buy her something!'

'Yeah. Well, I s'pose . . . I mean . . .' Sam waved a hand. 'As she's leaving, an' all.'

'You mean, we *ought* to buy her presents?' I knew that Sam was right. But I looked in my purse, and – Oh! I'd almost spent all my money.

Sam had almost spent hers, too. We'd spent it last week, on make-up. If we bought presents for Droopy, we wouldn't have enough left for modelling wax . . .

Sam heaved a sigh. 'I've told her, now. She'll be expecting something.'

What could we do? You can't not buy

someone a present when you've told them you're going to. It would be too cruel.

'Guess we'll have to,' said Sam.

So Sam bought an orange lipstick like the one she'd bought for herself last week; because old Droopy, she'd taken a real fancy to Sam's orange lipstick. She'd almost mashed it to a pulp, smearing it over her lips. I bought her an orange scrunchie for her hair and an orange bangle with sparkly bits. Then we bought some orange paper for wrapping them. Suddenly we'd got a thing about orange!

'How long have we been away?' I said.

'Not very long,' said Sam.

'Bout . . . half an hour?'

'Bout that.'

I was worried about Droopy. I wasn't sure she could manage to sit still for half an hour.

'Let's get her some doughnuts,' said Sam. 'She likes them.'

We spent the last of our money on jam

doughnuts and made our way back to the bench where we'd left Droopy. Guess what? She wasn't there!

'Where's she gone?' I wailed. 'I knew we shouldn't have left her!'

We ran all round the shopping centre, looking for that wretched girl. In and out of all the stores we'd been to the week before.

No sign of her! Then as we came out of HMV we bumped into the two Year 9s who'd talked to us last week.

'I don't s'ppose you've seen Dr – I mean, Ellen?' said Sam.

'Yeah, saw her just a while back. Why? You lost her?'

'We left her sitting on a bench. Where did you see her?'

'Heading out that way.' They pointed. 'Looked like she'd picked up a few boyfriends.'

'*Boy*friends?'

'Well . . . guys of some kind.'

Me and Sam stared at each other, aghast.

'Let's go!' said Sam.

We didn't hang about. We went charging off towards the exit.

'Why didn't they stop her?' I cried.

'Why couldn't she just stay put?' retorted Sam.

' 'Cos she can't! You know what she's like. We shouldn't ever have left her!'

If anything happened to Ellen, it would be all our fault.

# 8

We *streaked* out of that shopping centre. Even me. I was going so fast I thought my heart would explode. I could feel it, thumping away inside my chest . . . *ker PLOMP, ker PLOMP, ker PLOMP.* But I was determined to keep up with Sam!

We tore down the road, the big main road that goes out of town. It's six lanes wide, with traffic all roaring and belching. I'd never walked down there before; only been with Mum and Dad, in the car. You *can* walk. I mean there are pavements, and grass verges, and even scrubby patches of woodland. But I didn't like it.

I suppose I am a bit of a wimp. I get scared quite easily. If I hadn't been with Sam I think probably I would have gone running home to Mum, and Mum would have got the car out. Except that by then it might have been too late.

'Cos we spotted Droopy almost at once. She was further down the road, sitting on a seat. There were three boys with her. *Big* boys. They looked like they were trying to get her to go into the woods with them. I could see Droopy shaking her head and clutching the back of the seat.

'*Oi!*'

Sam didn't wait. She went charging towards them, waving her arms and shouting. And I charged with her! I didn't have time to be scared. I mean, I *was* scared; but I didn't have time to stop and think about it. I couldn't leave Sam to stand up to three big boys all on her own.

I don't know whether they would actually have done anything to poor old Droopy or whether they were just taunting her. I can't tell you the things they were saying. They are too horrible.

Poor old Droops was terrified. She was crying, and trying to cower away from them. And the boys were jeering and calling her names and going on about Droopy Drawers.

Maybe that was the moment I decided that we really oughtn't to be calling her Droopy. I think I made up my mind there and then that from now on she would be *Ellen*.

Sam told me afterwards that she'd come to the same decision.

'I just felt so awful. Thinking what might have happened to her. I mean, she shouldn't have been there with us, but . . . well!'

I knew what Sam meant. It wasn't Ellen's fault she was like she was. It was just the way things had turned out. It was up to me and Sam to keep a watch out for her – and we hadn't.

The boys had surrounded us. Their faces were all sneery. One of them said, 'Hi, kids! Want a bit of fun?'

I swallowed; but Sam, very fiercely, said, 'Ellen! It's time to go home.' And she grabbed her by the hand and hauled her up from the seat. The boys were grinning and making these rude gestures. I mean *really* rude gestures. Not like Charlie Potts and Gary Copestake. Theirs was just baby stuff. These boys were serious.

Me and Sam did our best to ignore them. I took out my hanky and gave it to Ellen, but she didn't seem to know what to do with it so I had to do it for her. I mopped her up and tried not to listen to what those horrible boys were saying.

They followed us all the way back to the shopping centre. Me and Sam had Ellen between us. Sam had hold of her arm and I had her hand. Ellen's hand was warm and soft, just like Ellen herself, and I suddenly felt incredibly bad about having called her Droopy and got mad at her.

'Ellen, don't cry!' I begged. We were nearly

there. The boys couldn't do anything to us now. 'Please, Ellen!'

It was getting to be an embarrassment. 'Cos when Ellen cried she didn't just cry, she *blubbed*. I mean, her whole face just crumpled up and drowned in an ocean of tears. People were starting to look at us like we'd done something to her. The boys had disappeared. As soon as we'd hit the shopping centre they'd gone swaggering off. So I suppose we must have looked a bit guilty, what with Sam hanging on to Ellen's arm and me clutching at her hand.

A woman stopped and gave us this really suspicious glare.

'Are you all right, dear?' she said to Ellen.

Ellen simply opened her mouth and howled even louder.

'We're taking her home,' said Sam.

'She got lost,' I added. It was sort of true. I mean, she had gone wandering off.

'Well, if you're sure,' said the woman. But

you could tell she didn't trust us, and I couldn't help noticing the way she looked at us, like she was fixing us in her memory so that later on, if anything happened, she'd be able to give the police our description. There was this tall dark girl with black hair and a little blonde one with a round face . . .

So embarrassing! But I reminded myself that Ellen was going home that afternoon and the main thing was, she was safe. But we couldn't take her back in this state!

'Let's go and clean her up,' I said to Sam.

So we took her into Hamlyn's, up to the Ladies on the third floor. The posh one! It's got hot-air dryers and little machines that spray you with perfume and other machines that spurt dollops of hand cream. Of course you have to put money in and we had hardly anything left, but we opened our purses and Sam managed to find 50p and I handed over my last £1 coin. And old Ellen, she put them in the machines and sprayed herself and spurted herself and was just so happy that the prospect of being dead broke for the whole of next week paled into insignificance. (I think that's the expression.)

After she'd finished spraying and spurting, and we'd washed her face and combed her hair with our fingers, we took her back down the escalator and out into the shopping centre, where we all sat on a bench and ate the doughnuts we'd bought. Those doughnuts really cheered her up! She was all beaming (and covered in sugar). It was like we'd never found her cowering on the seat and crying her eyes out.

'We've got your presents here,' I said. 'But they're for later,' I added quickly, as Ellen reached out a hand. 'We haven't wrapped them yet.'

'And you don't deserve them anyway,' scolded Sam. 'Going off like that! I thought we told you to stay put!'

Ellen munched on her doughnut.

'We told you to wait for us! Didn't we?'

'Forgot?' said Ellen.

'Forgot?'

I wondered why Sam was bothering. It wasn't any use expecting Ellen to give you sensible answers. She wasn't a sensible kind of person! She did things without thinking. She couldn't tell you *why* she did them: she just did them.

But Sam persisted. She can be really stubborn.

'Why'd you go off like that?'

'Was it the boys?' I said.

Ellen thought about it. She was busy sucking jam from her fingers. Noisily. Like she was making all these little pops and squeaks.

'Did they come and talk to you?'

'Mmm.' She nodded.

'Are they from your year?'

She thought about it again and slowly shook her head.

'But you do know them?'

'No.' Ellen slurped, busily, at her fingers.

'You don't even *know* them?' said Sam. 'So why did you go with them?'

'They said they were going to show me something.'

'Show you what?'

'They wouldn't tell me. They said I'd got to go with them and then they'd show me.'

Sam and me exchanged looks. Hadn't Ellen been taught that you should never go off with strangers? Especially great yobbish ones like that.

'Ellen,' I said, 'you shouldn't *ever* go off with people you don't know.'

'But they said they were going to show me something!'

'And you *believed* them?' said Sam.

Ellen was starting to look frightened.

'They told me,' she whispered.

'It doesn't make any difference,' said Sam. 'You don't *know* them.'

143

'Even if you did,' I said, 'you oughtn't to have gone with them.'

'They could have hurt you,' said Sam.

Ellen's lips began to quiver. Quickly, before she could start crumpling again, I said, 'It doesn't matter this time 'cos me and Sam were there. But you mustn't ever, ever, do it again. Not ever.'

Ellen sniffed, miserably. Her eyes were already filling with tears.

'We're not mad at you,' said Sam. 'It's just . . . well! We care about you, see? We don't want anything happening to you.'

'Won't do it again,' mumbled Ellen.

'Do you promise?' I said.

'I do! I promise! I promise, I promise! I pr—'

'Ok,' said Sam. 'Just so long as you remember.'

'I will, I will, IwillIwillIwill!'

'Next time a stranger asks you to go anywhere, you got to say to yourself, *remember what Sam and Abi said.*'

'Remember what Sam and Abi said.'

'Right!'

'Remember what Sam and Abi said, remember what S—'

'Say it *inside* yourself,' I said. 'That way, it'll sink in better.'

'All the way home, she said it inside herself. I could see her lips moving as she hopped on and off the kerb. As we turned into our road we bumped into Her Next Door. Mrs Pink. She took one look at Ellen hopping, and snapped, 'That's no way for a grown girl to walk down the road!'

It wasn't, of course, but I didn't see what business it was of hers. If Ellen wanted to hop, why shouldn't she hop? It wasn't hurting anyone. There wasn't any traffic.

Sam obviously felt as indignant as I did.

'It's a new way of keeping fit,' she said. 'Kerb hopping. They do it all the time in America.'

Next thing I know, Sam's madly hopping

on and off the kerb herself, and I'm doing it as well, and Her Next Door's waddling off down the road in a right old rage. I expect she'll complain to Mum that we've cheeked her, but I don't care!

And old Ellen, she looks at us, very solemn, and goes, 'Remember what Sam and Abi said.'

'You've got it!' cries Sam, and thumps her on the back. And old Ellen beams this big banana beam, stretching from ear to ear. She's dead chuffed, you can tell. She's done something right. At last!

That afternoon, Miss Davies arrived with Ellen's mum. We were surprised, 'cos she was really pleasant-looking. I think we'd both been expecting someone a bit . . . well! Plain and bag-like. Which just goes to show, as Mum is always telling us. You should wait till you meet people and not pass judgement on them.

Ellen was overjoyed to be with her mum

again! That surprised us a bit as well, 'cos we hadn't thought she cared. But the minute she saw her, she hurled herself at her and flung both arms round her neck. Her mum was pretty happy too. She even had tears in her eyes!

How's my little girl?' she said.

It sounds kind of soppy, I know, but honestly it wasn't. It was really touching. I found I almost had tears in my eyes, too! So did Sam, though she tried to hide it. But I know she did 'cos she sniffed and wiped her nose on the back of her sleeve.

The Radish just stood there, owly-eyed. He was too young to take it all in.

See, what was so touching was Ellen's mum calling her 'my little girl' when in fact she was quite big and lumping. But because we knew Ellen, we could understand why her mum called her that. She was so innocent and trusting! You just felt you wanted to protect her. I guess that's what her mum felt, too.

'I am so grateful to you,' she told Mum. 'And to – Sam, isn't it? And Abi? And Gus? Thank you so much for taking care of my Ellen for me!'

'It's been a pleasure,' said Mum. She turned to me and Sam. 'Hasn't it, girls?'

We agreed that it had. We'd suddenly forgotten all the times she'd embarrassed us!

'Ellen.' Her mum pushed her forward. 'Are you going to say thank you to Mrs Foster for looking after you? And Abi, and Sam, and Gus?'

Ellen said, 'Thank you, Mrs Foster.' *Mwah!* Big kiss. 'Thank you, Abi.' Kiss. 'Thank you, Sam!' Kiss. 'Thank you, Gus!' Kiss.

She kissed each of us in turn, including the animals. 'Thank you, Daisy ! Thank you, Jack! Thank you, Felix!'

'And here are your presents,' I said, when she'd finished. We'd done them up in funny shapes so she wouldn't be able to guess what they were. 'But you're not to open them till you get home!'

'Well, aren't you a lucky girl?' said Ellen's mum. 'And we've got something for Sam and Abi! And for Gus. Do you want to give them to them?'

Ellen grabbed, eagerly. 'I'll give them, I'll give them!'

Out of her bag her mum produced three envelopes, which Ellen solemnly handed to us.

'Here's your present, Abi. Here's your present, Sam. Here's your present, Gus. Now open them, quickly, and let's see what they are!'

Ellen's mum had bought us gift vouchers. Brilliant! On Sunday we could go into Hamlyn's and spend them! I said this to Ellen's mum, and *that* was a *big* mistake!

'Me too, me too!' clamoured Ellen at once. 'I'll come with you!'

Just for a moment, we froze; but then her

mum said it was time they were leaving.

'I hate to drag you away, but we really ought to be going. From the sound of things, you've had a wonderful time!'

'I have, I have!' said Ellen, doing one of her twirls. 'I wish Sam and Abi could come and live with us!'

'Well, maybe,' suggested her mum, 'they could come and visit some time. We could invite them to tea.'

'Yessssssssssss!' Ellen really liked that idea. She flew at us and kissed us again. 'Come to tea, come to tea!'

Sam and me promised that we would.

'We'd love to,' I said.

As I said it, I thought, 'Maybe she'll forget.' But the funny thing was, when Ellen and her mum had gone off with Miss Davies and the door had closed behind them, the house suddenly felt most peculiar and empty. And I realised that in an odd kind of way I was going to miss Ellen. I'd miss her big beaming face across the breakfast table every morning. I'd miss her hoppity-skipping on and off the kerb on the way to school. I'd even miss her bursting in on me and Sam uninvited and hurling herself down on to one of our beds, showing all her knickers.

Sam admitted that she felt the same. I suppose what it was, we'd grown kind of used to her.

'But it will be nice to have my bedroom back again,' I said.

'Yeah, and it'll be nice not to have you nagging at me all the time,' said Sam.

We rushed upstairs and began carting Sam's stuff back into her own room.

'D'you think she will invite us to tea?' I said.

'Dunno,' said Sam.

'We'd have to go,' I said, 'wouldn't we?'

'Yeah. It'd only be polite.'

'I wouldn't actually *mind*,' I said.

Sam agreed that she wouldn't mind, either.

'It'd be quite fun, seeing old Droopy again.'

We were back to calling her Droopy. But it was different from the way we'd called her Droopy before. Now we did it 'cos we were fond of her.

'I hope she remembers,' I said.

'If she doesn't,' said Sam, 'we'll remind her!'

*Jean Ure*

*Book 1: My Sister Sam*

Abi's always wanted a sister, so when her parents announce they're going to foster Sam, Abi is thrilled! And Sam is brilliant – bright, bubbly, and larger than life. Abi just knows they're going to be the best of friends.

But when Sam starts giving everyone expensive gifts, Abi is suspicious. Where is the money coming from? Abi really wants to think the best of Sam, but some things you just can't ignore . . .

*Jean Ure*

*Book 2: Meet the Radish*

Abi and Sam are going to have a brother! They're not mad on boys on the whole, but little Gus is adorable. He's only six, with a crop of carrot-red hair. Sam and Abi call him 'the Radish'.

The Radish is shy, and *really* timid, but pretty soon the girls can't imagine life without him. Then his real mum turns up – and everything is spoilt . . .

*Jean Ure*

**Book 4: Secret Simon**

Abi and Sam argue sometimes but at least they agree on one thing – boys are GROSS. Well, most of them, the Radish doesn't count – he's only little.

Then Simon arrives and everything changes. He's drop-dead gorgeous and can charm the birds out of the trees. Simon's got everyone wrapped round his little finger. All except Sam. She doesn't trust him. Not one bit. Nobody's THAT perfect!

*The Foster Family*

## ORDER FORM

| | | | |
|---|---|---|---|
| 0 340 72721 7 | 1: MY SISTER SAM | £3.99 | ❏ |
| 0 340 72722 5 | 2: MEET THE RADISH | £3.99 | ❏ |
| 0 340 72724 1 | 3: SECRET SIMON | £3.99 | ❏ |

*All Hodder Children's books are available at your local bookshop, or can be ordered direct from the publisher. Just tick the titles you would like and complete the details below. Prices and availability are subject to change without prior notice.*

Please enclose a cheque or postal order made payable to *Bookpoint Ltd*, and send to: Hodder Children's Books, 39 Milton Park, Abingdon, OXON OX14 4TD, UK.
Email Address: orders@bookpoint.co.uk

If you would prefer to pay by credit card, our call centre team would be delighted to take your order by telephone. Our direct line *01235 400414* (lines open 9.00 am–6.00 pm Monday to Saturday, 24 hour message answering service). Alternatively you can send a fax on *01235 400454*.

| TITLE | | FIRST NAME | | SURNAME | |
|---|---|---|---|---|---|
| ADDRESS | | | | | |
| | | | | | |
| | | | | | |
| DAYTIME TEL: | | | POST CODE | | |

If you would prefer to pay by credit card, please complete:
Please debit my Visa/Access/Diner's Card/American Express (delete as applicable) card no:

| | | | | | | | | | | | | | | | | | |
|--|--|--|--|--|--|--|--|--|--|--|--|--|--|--|--|--|--|
| | | | | | | | | | | | | | | | | | |

Signature ..................................................... Expiry Date: ..............................

If you would NOT like to receive further information on our products please tick the box. ❏